June and her sister, lyn, are NDNs—real ones.

lyn has her pottery artwork, her precocious kid, Willow, and the uncertain terrain of her midlife to keep her mind, heart and hands busy. June, a Métis Studies professor, yearns to uproot from Vancouver and move. With her loving partner, Sigh, and their faithful pup, June decides to buy a house in the last place on earth she imagined she'd end up: back home in Winnipeg with her family.

But then into lyn and June's busy lives a bomb drops: their estranged and very white mother, Renee, is called out as a "pretendian." Under the name (get this) Raven Bearclaw, Renee had topped the charts in the Canadian art world, winning awards and recognition for her Indigenous-style work.

The news is quickly picked up by the media and sparks an enraged online backlash. As the sisters are pulled into the painful tangle of lies their mother has told and the hurt she has caused, searing memories from their unresolved childhood trauma, which still manages to spill into their well-curated adult worlds, come rippling to the surface.

In prose so powerful it could strike a match, *real ones* is written with the same signature wit and heart on display in *The Break*, *The Strangers* and *The Circle*. An energetic, probing and ultimately hopeful story, *real ones* pays homage to the long-fought, hard-won battles of Michif (Métis) people to regain ownership of their identity and the right to say who is and isn't Métis.

advance praise for *real ones*

"With the same artistry and open heart that vermette's character lyn practices in throwing and displaying her pottery, vermette has crafted *real ones* to explore—in real time—the traumatic outward rippling effect of a mother's ethnic fraud on all her relations."

—Michelle Good, author of *Five Little Indians* and *Truth Telling*

"A brilliant novel, infused with anger and rich with empathy. In *real ones*, katherena vermette holds a mirror up to an issue that Indigenous and non-Indigenous communities are all grappling with—the rise of false claims to Indigenous identity. vermette tells this story like no one else can. By focusing on the relationship between sisters June and lyn (who are Métis on their father's side) following the public discovery of their own mother's false claims, vermette offers up an understanding of the way the phenomenon reverberates at the personal and political levels. A healing and eye-opening story, *real ones* is a must-read."

—Michelle Porter, author of *A Grandmother Begins the Story*

praise for katherena vermette

"[vermette] is among the most gifted and relevant writers of our time." —David Chariandy, author of *Brother*

"A tremendously gifted writer, a dazzling talent."
—Madeleine Thien, author of *Do Not Say We Have Nothing*

"[vermette] creates unforgettable characters with honour, respect, and a deft hand." —Lee Maracle, author of *Celia's Song*

"A staggering talent."
—Eden Robinson, author of *Monkey Beach*

real ones

a novel

katherena vermette

HAMISH HAMILTON
an imprint of Penguin Canada, a division of Penguin Random House
Canada Limited

Canada • USA • UK • Ireland • Australia • New Zealand • India •
South Africa • China

First published 2024

LIBRARY AND ARCHIVES CANADA CATALOGUING IN PUBLICATION

Title: Real ones : a novel / Katherena Vermette.
Names: Vermette, Katherena, 1977- author.
Identifiers: Canadiana (print) 20240357698 | Canadiana (ebook)
  20240357728 | ISBN 9780735247505 (hardcover) |
  ISBN 9780735247512 (EPUB)
Subjects: LCGFT: Novels.
Classification: LCC PS8643.E74 R43 2024 | DDC C813/.6—dc23

Book design by Jen Griffiths
Typeset by Sean Tai
Cover design by Jen Griffiths
Cover image © Julie Flett

Printed in Canada

10 9 8 7 6 5 4 3 2 1

Penguin
Random House
HAMISH HAMILTON CANADA

for all my sisters—Ceremony, street, soul, spirit—you've kept me up. I love you.

Chi Maarsii

Truth is like water—it finds a way.

MICHELLE GOOD, author of
Five Little Indians and *Truth Telling*

Contents

1

real ones

lyn

There are many ways to make a clay vessel. Lately, I've been making pinch pot style. Deceptively simple, pinch pots are made from balls of clay dented in the middle by a thumb or finger, then shaped around and around until the sides flatten and it starts to resemble something like a bowl. They can be small or large, but I keep mine contained to my hand so relatively small. I smooth and wet the clay over and delicately over again (so many times). Cracks are pushed together, edges pinched. Sometimes I use rocks or shells or bone to carve and form, add, decorate. It's methodical work that requires mindfulness and constant return to presentness. I think most, if not all, art does.

I am working on a series of vessels like this. Small bowls made in the way of our ancestors, the very old peoples we don't even have names for. We don't know what they called themselves but they are still here. We are them.

So much about North America's original peoples has been forcibly silenced (nothing new there), but they wrote messages to us in the earth, with the earth. Teachings we can learn from, dig up, find them and in them, ourselves. Things like how to make a small clay bowl. Something so everyday but sacred at the same time.

Ancient folks made many kinds of vessels like these and different, various shapes and sizes. They held water, were cooking pots, held all sorts of food within. In a pinch (ha!) they could also be used to place harvested plants, grains and seeds. Something for a child to play with.

The clay is made from the earth itself. Right here at our feet, usually from riverbanks or wet marshy places. Formed then fired, and then when done with, buried in the earth. Returned. That is where we find them now. That is where our Teachings literally lie. What I am trying to re-create.

I am learning as much as I can. From an archaeologist at the museum, from Elders, the Internet, stitching knowledges back together. Weaving some small part of all they knew. All they would have wanted us to know.

It is a healing. It's not without healing. It is healing a part of myself that was broken before I was even born.

I am still working on all the parts that got ripped apart after.

At some point last night, I had called June and said, "I think I've been depressed all summer.
I mean I thought I was over Shannon
but it's been so hard not having Willow here."

She said, "I think you've been depressed as long as I've known you."

June is trying to be funny. She's my sister. Two years older.

When I work, hours pass. I dip my cramped hands into the water and massage the clay from moment to moment. I leave the window open to the birds singing in the old elm trees outside. Hear snippets of conversation as people go by on the sidewalk. Otherwise, it is just me and my art and thoughts. I make a vessel. I finish it and set it down. I don't stop. Only grab a new ball and push my fingers into the formless mound, wondering where to start.

I should have started already. I am filled with the anxiety of beginning.

Maybe I have already begun.

June

I am going to miss the mountains, the ocean, the tall tall trees. The muffled noises of the city in the rain.

My dog Zeke and I cross 6th and turn down our narrow little street. Cars parked on either side and oversized houses tower overhead. This place has always made me feel slightly claustrophobic.

I am not going to miss this apartment. A mouldy basement suite in a rundown house was never going to be my favourite. But it has a shared greenspace, is in Kits, has a tiny alcove I made into an office. Pretty good, considering Vancouver housing, but I never liked it. Not all the way. I am not going to miss it at all.

My stomach leaps at the sight of Sigh's truck. Wedged between a rusty hatchback and a brand new EV, so tight I wonder how he got in, how he'll get out. I look down at my phone, but no, he didn't message to say he'd be home.

There was a missed call from Renee though. I am not about to call her back just now. I am stressed enough already. Do not need to talk to my mother, too.

"Hey?" I call from the doorway.

"Hey you. I had a headache. It was a slow day anyway." He has his excuses annoyingly prepared.

I find my husband in the kitchen, eating leftovers out of a container. He still smiles when I walk into the room, even with a full mouth. I unhook Zeke's leash and my Lab greets his other human for a quick second before going to town on his water bowl.

"Have you taken a painkiller?" I ask him.

"Yes, Doctor." Mouth still full.

"Fuck off." More joking than mean.

"Love you." He puts the container back in the fridge, didn't close the lid all the way.

I exhale. "What are you going to do, then?"

"I'm going to take a nap, see how I feel. What are you up to?"

I inhale, feel it all: "Gotta pack. Gotta call the bank about the line of credit. Did you check on the trailer rental?"

"Yeh, it's all sorted."

"Are you sure? 'Cause sometimes those reservations don't stick. We need a trailer. It won't all fit in your truck."

"I know."

"I think you should double-check."

"I think it will be fine."

"I think you're not taking this seriously."

"I think you're anxious and finding things to be anxious about."

"I think we're moving across the country in like, days and you're not being anxious enough."

"I think you should have a nap with me."

"Fuck off." A little meaner than I meant to be.

"So much!" He kisses the top of my head and turns to go to the bedroom. Takes his shirt off as he goes. His dark back muscles always make me forget how annoyed I am. For a minute, anyway.

Moving is not really a big deal for us, we move all the time, but this time we bought a house. A whole actual house. In Winnipeg. My hometown. Sigh's from out here. We've been all over, lived all over, but never back home. I've only been back for visits since I went away for school and would have never went back to live, but Sigh wanted to. Wanted to buy a house. Stop moving around for a while. Be grownups.

He was/is so excited about it. Had hounded the agent with multiple video tours, politely and nervously asked my dad to go by and check it, twice. It took weeks for him to finally make an offer. Well, "we" made an offer but it was mostly him. Downright cheap by our standards, coming from out here where we never even thought about buying anything.

Our first-ever bought house is an older two-storey with an attic not far from my sister lyn's. Good part of the West End. I've always loved her street, so full of elms and cozy wartime houses. Our new house is different though, older than most around there, and bigger. Three floors. So much space. It has a living room and dining room on the right, staircase on the left, three bedrooms upstairs, large attic space. I sort of remember living in a house like that but I was very small. I only remember the wood rail on the stairs, walking up all by myself. Maybe it wasn't our house.

Grandma Genie was there, in the memory, but I don't know if she lived there or was visiting. It wasn't the brown house where we lived with Mamere Annie and everybody, I know that for sure.

I'll have to ask Dad about it.

Sigh naps and I go through my things to do: text my niece Willow, to remind her about the moving plan and check in. See how she's doing. She's out here for a summer program at the university. Was nervous and shy at first but really seems to have settled in well. Is not replying today. I've learned this is a good sign.

I call the bank about money. Am on hold way too long. I have to pack. I should be packing. I should go through my books.

But instead, I check my socials, go into emails. My phone plays an instrumental rendition of "Smells Like Teen Spirit" for the eighth time. The first time I was embarrassed for myself, then I was annoyed, by this time though, I am singing along when a subject line stops me. Dead.

"Raven Bearclaw."

Oh fuck.

lyn

My sister reads it out to me. I put my phone on speaker and work the clay as she goes:

"Dear Dr. Stranger-Savage,

"Hello. I am Mr. Not Important, a reporter working with the Globe newsgroup. I am doing a story on an artist named Raven Bearclaw and have come to understand that this is a pseudonym for your mother, Renee Stranger. I've been working on this story for months now. We've done a full genealogy and taken statements from communities she's claimed to be a part of. Perhaps it will come as a shock to you that her dubious claims of Indigenous ancestry have been proven to be completely unfounded and she seems to have no connection to any of the Métis or Mi'kmaq communities she has named over the years.

"I would love to talk more with you about this, if you can get back to me at your earliest convenience. I do plan to publish very soon.

"Sincerely, Who Cares"

June inhales loud. Her breath seems to wobble, but I scoff: "Wow. Mr. Who Cares sounds like a real a-hole."

"He's not wrong." She's worried.

"It has nothing to do with us."

"That's naive. We're gonna be pulled into this like a riptide." She's so worried.

"Like a what?" Sincere question.

"Riptide.

"Riptide?"

"It's a fucking ocean, tide . . . you're not *that* fucking prairie!"

"Stop swearing. *Riptide.* What are you, a surfer now?" I am trying to make her laugh. I feel this, this need to lighten things.

"Fuck off."

"I always wanted to try surfing." I keep smoothing at the clay, keep dipping my fingers in the water, keep it soft and wet in my palm. I love the way it forms to my skin, my bones. However my hand is shaped, it shapes like that.

"Well get out of the fucking prairies and maybe you can." So agitated. (To be fair, June is almost always agitated.)

"*You* get out of the prairies. You're the one moving back here. We're like the mob, hey?" I laugh.

"The what?"

"The mob. You keep 'trying to get out . . .'" I do my best Brando but she's not lightening up. I can feel her edges across the provinces, through the phone. "You're worrying too much. This is just another Renee thing in a lifetime of Renee things. It will blow over and it's not on us. Not our circus. Not our monkeys."

"Whatever, Ms. Therapized. This shit sticks. Everyone is going to think we're pretendians, too."

"No, they're not. And if they do, to hell with 'em. We got cards. We got community. In a pinch, we can sic Grandma Genie on them. We're good." I laugh and imagine my aged Grandma in one of her favourite polyester pant suits (mauve) attacking like a pit bull. (She could totally take you, don't even try.)

"Nothing about this is even close to good. I just got this job. They could pull my contract if they even think—"

"They're not going to pull your contract."

"They could."

"Pfft."

I should explain (ahem), our mother Renee is a pretendian (fake NDN), goes by the name Raven Bearclaw (can't make this stuff up). My sister and I are Michif via my dad's family, also called Métis, also called Red River Métis, also called you know the *not fake* ones.

More accurately (in my view), Renee is an artist and very stereotypical in her way of being that kind of artist type person, she takes on impersonates embodies reinvents herself by the season (or mood).

One of her current illusions, to herself or otherwise, is that she is Indigenous. But she isn't. Or at least I don't think she is. As far as I know or have always known, she is Mennonite and French. French from Quebec. That's all we've ever known. Dad too, and they met when they were kids, were married for a decade. None of us ever heard anything about her being Métis until a few years ago, including her sister Adele, who in her signature Aunty Dell way called the whole thing "another one of Renee's loads of horseshit."

June and I are quiet for a beat. I smooth the round rim and try, "Did you say this shit *sticks*? Like not stinks but sticks?"

"Stop trying to be funny."

"No trying about it. I'm hilarious." I exaggerate a laugh.

She sighs. June always lets me get my way. Eventually. It's like I can hear her half smile. "Yeh, it sticks, like sticks on us. This shit."

"I thought you said stinks." I finish my vessel and put it down. Look at it. Happy with it. They are all so different. Have their own personality. I can tell them apart like a mother can always tell her children from one another. Will always know this one I made when it all started. When I pretended not to care and reassure my sister that it was okay that Renee, who had absolutely no Indigenous anything ever, had been pretending to for years. (Some of the straight up facts I have said about my life are *straight up* crazy.)

"It stinks too."

"Does."

Renee always dressed up like an NDN, but she dressed up like a lot of things and we never thought anything of it. Questionable misappropriating things, sure, but in the eighties, nineties everyone did that (oos, too). I remember her wearing bindis, kimonos, was obsessed with those Chinese traditional shirts for a while, would always come back from somewhere with that somewhere's accent. Loved a good batik scarf! When I started high school, she was a part of an Afro drum group led by a white guy named

Kevin from Windsor, Ontario (yes, really). At one point, when I was super young, she was a belly dancer (?!). Posing as Métis ("metis") is not a big stretch.

She's an artist you know, those people be crazy.

June riles herself up again. "I'm going to call Aunty Dell. We should draft a statement. Get ahead of this, as he says."

"Draft a statement! We're not on trial here. And Aunty Dell hasn't talked to *her* either. *She* doesn't talk to anyone anymore apparently, except you."

"But they might contact Aunty too. She should know and we should, you know, draft a mutual statement."

"Saying what exactly?"

"I don't even know."

"Did you talk to *her*? What does she say about this?" I press my palms into the table. The leftover clay stiffens as it starts to dry on the back of my hands.

"I don't know. She called. I'm afraid to call her back now."

"You should probably do that."

"I don't want to. I wish you would."

"Yeh, that's not going to happen."

"You should email this reporter then. You do that, I'll talk to Renee."

"Why do we have to do *any*thing?"

"We just do!" she snaps. "When it happened that last time, she said it was *nothing*. Just 'jealous people, nothing, nothing,' right?"

"Well, there you go then. Obviously that's the right answer. She has a such a firm grip on reality." I submerge my hands in the cold water and grab a fresh ball.

It was a few years ago, Renee told June this story that she found out her Grandpa, our Great-Grandpa, was a Shaman. Métis *and* a Shaman.

It sounded like a ludicrous story in a long line of ludicrous stories and situations. I ignored it at first, didn't think anything would happen with it. I hadn't talked or had anything to do with her for years at that point. Didn't think it concerned me.

But then this artist named (wait for it) Raven Bearclaw! won all these awards. I had heard of her but never seen her. She was the new toast of Canadian art, apparently, literally remaking the entirety of the Woodlands tradition (style of painting). "Saviour" was the word on the headline next to a picture of Renee with dyed black hair and a bad spray tan. She had her thinking seriously look on—the one she gave me when she was most disappointed in my behaviour, back when I was really young and she gave a shit about my behaviour. She was wearing a south west–style turquoise necklace and her trademark Guatemalan orange wrap she would tell you was handmade for her by village craftsmen outside of Tikal.

Back then I freaked out: "Where did she get this Shaman stuff from?" I had asked my sister.

"I dunno. She just said 'Shaman.' Her Grandpa from Quebec."

"He married an Indigenous woman? That doesn't make her Métis. That's not what that means."

"No, she wasn't Indigenous. They both had French names and lineage. That's what Aunty Dell said she knew. But what do I know."

"So you think this is true? Like could be true?"

"No, I think it's flimsy as hell, but I work in academia—you can't shoot an arrow without hitting a pretendian in a university."

"What are we going to do?!"

"What can we do?" It's like I felt her shrug through the phone. She was in Australia at the time. I think she felt far enough away from it.

Unfortunately, I felt very close to it. Went through all the emotions. Landing longest on shocked appalled livid. I wanted to break things, couldn't sit still. I told all my friends. Everyone I knew in the art world. I told gallery owners, wrote a grant provider I knew who had sponsored one of her awards. How could you don't you know what the hell.

Well actually Shannon, being my loving, more sensible partner at the time, wrote those more official emails, articulated them so much better than I could have. They're a lawyer. They write good letters. Real good at talking shit and making it sound sweet.

But nothing happened. I didn't have a name anyone would recognize. Never was that great at actually effecting change. Some people responded with a half-arsed "thank you for bringing this to our attention. We will consider . . ." but mostly I was ignored.

They all probably thought I was jealous and nuts, fine. I let it go eventually (yeh, right), calmed down at least (gave up). What else could I do? Let the art world have her, then.

I mean, her name was Raven Bearclaw. If you believe that then you deserve what you get.

"This is bad, lyn. This is it! It's going to be big and it's going to fall on us like it always does."

"When did she say Mi'kmaq? I only knew about the pseudo-Métis stuff."

"I don't know."

I laugh. "It's crazy this is. It does stick. It sticks so hard." The sheer levels of my humour (so many levels).

"Fuck off." June sighs.

I sigh back. Say honestly (only for a minute), "We should tell Dad. And Willow. I should definitely tell my kid about this."

"We should tell everyone. We should have when this all started."

"I know. We're horrible people."

"Fuck off."

I can't email the reporter. I don't trust what I'll say. I don't have Shannon around anymore to make it sound better.

June

When I get off the phone, Sigh, who heard everything from across the hall, comes in with a sympathetic look and a "You okay?"

I want to say something funny, laugh it off like lyn does, but it fills all the way up too fast. Too much. I shake my head but still start to cry. No, burst. It's a burst.

Sigh reaches out for me. Holds on tight. My body shakes in his strong arms for a long time.

After I catch my breath, he takes Zeke outside with his phone and vape, claiming with that flirty smile he'll call the trailer company. I know he's just being kind but I appreciate it.

I take a deep breath and check the time. Won't be too late in Montreal. She's a night person like my sister anyway.

"Hey, Renee."
    "Oh honey, honey. I am so glad to hear your voice, you wouldn't believe the day I am having. The worst, just unimaginable."
    "Yeh, I can, imagine. This reporter emailed me—"

"It's such a . . . oh I am so . . . it's such BS, Juneybug. You wouldn't believe. This is a witch hunt. I am being persecuted. It's all this one artist, this one jealous little insignificant little, well she's a bitch, pardon my French, no other way about it. She's still moping about a grant I got and she didn't or something. Childish is what it is."

"It's not one person, Renee. These accusations—"

"Everyone is talking out their asses. Just jumping on the cancel culture bandwagon. It's all so typical. They don't know their history."

"I think you should . . . I wonder if you apologize . . ."

"Apologize! Me? For what? I haven't done anything wrong. My only mistake is being successful. No, I am not apologizing to anyone. No way. After all this? This is abuse is what this is."

I don't want to say anything more. I wish I could hang up and stare at my books. Pack them. Have a quiet night.

Frustrated: "All I did was speak my truth. No one can say anything about *my* truth."

I speak quietly, slowly. Trying. "They did a genealogy . . ."

Exasperated: "Oh my girl, you don't understand. People will cut you down as soon as they see you make something of yourself. They want to see me fail!"

"I don't think that's what this is—"

Angry, again: "They know nothing. I've done my own research. You don't know what I've been through with this."

I'm so tired all of a sudden. I want to curl up on the couch. I want to close my eyes and sleep.

"I was married to your dad for nearly eleven years, that ought to count for something. I mean I know what I'm talking about."

I speak slow, more for my tired self than to be gentle to her: "Being married to an Indigenous person is not the same as being an Indigenous person."

She scoffs and moves on quick: "Now the university, *my* university, is threatening to end my contract, can you believe that? I should sue this reporter for slander is what I should do. Sue him and that uppity dean believing his . . . I have worked there for years!"

"You have to prove slander," I say but she's not stopping.

"She should be falling over herself protecting me but no, she's too worried about being politically correct and her precious dean job. I mean, she can't fire me! That's illegal!"

I stare at my books, read the spines. Wait it out.

"Just don't say anything, Juneybug. Don't say anything and it will all go away. They'll go find someone else to try and cancel, these do-gooders." She finally takes a breath.

Stupidly, I try again. "He says he's publishing soon."

"You're not going to talk to him, are you? You're not thinking of that! Would you really? Would you really do that for me? Speak to him for me?"

"I can't like, defend this, Renee. I don't know . . ."

"Oh, you are right about that one, you don't know!" She checks herself, and her voice softens. "You don't understand, Juneybug, my girl, and I really think, no I know, you should keep quiet. If you're not going to stand up for me, then fine. Fine. Then just do what you've done and do nothing."

She never used to call me "my girl." My sister neither. Something she's picked up recently. Never sounds right.

I make some excuse for having to go and I hang up. I knew I should have said something more, kept trying, but couldn't. I tell myself it's because she wouldn't listen. And she wouldn't've, but that doesn't mean I shouldn't've kept trying.

But I do nothing. Nothing less than what I have always done.

I do know though. I know all of it. I have degrees in this stuff, three of them and a post-bacc. Michif/Métis history, literature, Native studies. Canada, the US, Australia. Ten years of full-time study before I started teaching. Now I teach, write academic articles, constantly research everything surrounding contemporary Indigenous identity, and our history and ethnogenesis. That's how much I understand. How much I know.

Sigh comes back in with the dog. I lie down on the couch and Zeke curls up with me. My husband picks up my feet and sits in the corner. Turns on a movie we both don't watch.

Before tonight, I hadn't talked to Renee in over six months. She had called me back then to invite me to a gallery show she was in: "It's going to be the toast of the town, Juneybug. It would mean so much to me if you could show up for me. I would just love that."

"When is it?" I know I was doing something at the time. Probably cleaning. Not really paying attention.

"Next Thursday."

I stopped. "Renee, I can't fly across the country in less than a week."

"I don't see why not, you seem to go to Winnipeg all the time."

"I don't . . . When I go home, it's planned, way ahead of time, and during school breaks. My term just started."

"Oh, I should've known better asking any of you to support me." She paused for effect and a tone change. "You know, if you could make a post about it, that would mean a lot. You have so many followers these days. A post would go a long way."

"I have maybe two hundred followers? If that. I never go on anymore."

"I always see you posting about Native stuff."

"Sovereignty and environmental issues maybe. The odd time."

"It would be nice to get your support. For a change. That would be nice."

I didn't post anything. Didn't even look it up. Knowing me, I probably didn't even go on any of my socials for days. Too scared that she'd tag me or message or somehow convince me to.

I know this is cowardly. How I've kept my head in the sand. But ignorance is the only way I've been able to stay in touch with her.

I didn't just make an excuse for having to go. Renee had begged me. She started crying and said, "Please Juneybug, please don't do what I think you're going to do. Don't say something silly and ruin me. If you're not going to support me, then just say nothing. All this time you've said nothing, you haven't supported me or anything, so don't be like this now. Please. It'll blow over, I promise. Just do this for me, just this once. I never ask for anything, do I?"

I said, "Okay." It was a whisper. I don't know why I said it. I didn't mean it. I only wanted to get off the phone.

2

strong female lead

lyn

Too early in the morning texts:

Dad—I'll be ther later. fix your sink.

Aunty Dell—Make your Scrabble move already. I got a bloody bingo I wanna use. [crying laughing emoji]

Grandma Genie—Are you still coming to visit this wek? My cousins grandsons girlfriend dropped off pickerel yesterday. Too much for me to eat. [long line of emojis, including various colours of hearts, a couple fish and several peaches] (She doesn't know the other meaning of the peach emoji—don't know where she picked that up.)

My kid, Willow (from late the night before. Still too early over there for her)—Only one week left. I can't believe it. I love it here!!

And then—If it fits, I sits. [cat meme] (She knows me so well.)

My baby sister, Yoyo—I can't believe they're going to be here in a week. A week!!! (She also passed along a couple vids but they weren't of animals so hardly worth mentioning.)

I didn't want to get out of bed. Couldn't sleep then slept in. My head ached. My bones grieved. Kept my eyes shut to my bright purple bedroom walls Shannon had painted years ago, tried not to feel the soft expensive sheets (Valentine's present).

Shannon who could speak their language. Shannon who was so smart and put together. Shannon who loved me for years and years and then stopped.

I had been dreaming of my old cat. Shannon's cat. We got him together, but they took him when they left. A rescue, of course. About two or three years old they figured. Walter. He got fat quick so he was likely young.

He humped my leg as I slept. I kept waking up to a very firm calf massage. I had to kick him off. Shannon thought I was being mean. He never humped them. (Yes, he was fixed.) He would sit in the sun with me sometimes. Reluctantly let me pet him occasionally but never cuddled. He only went downstairs to the basement to shit while I was working, stared at me as he did it.

Since they left, I've only seen him in pictures they've posted. Their engagement announcement. Some random couple photos. The long shot of their living room redo. The cat looked content.

I hope he humps their wife.

I finally get up, turn on the coffee and stand there impatient for it to brew. Count the clouds out my kitchen window—a habit that came from anxious passing of time, something suggested to help me be calm, be present. Me trying to be in the present moment all the time like I was supposed to.

> I breathe into the day and feel my feelings, like the
> books told me to, like my therapist gently reminds me
> to. Feel my feelings
> in short, achievable increments.

> > Try to believe I can feel them and won't die.
> > That they will pass
> > and I will not die.
> > they will not kill me

No, I lie
I'm not being mindful at all
I'm wallowing.

I wait for coffee then sip coffee then angrily stare out the window nosing at my neighbours who are painting a stupid colour on their stupid house looking all stupid in love and coupled up and summery and shit and I feel sorry for myself. Wallowing.

I like to joke that as an artist feeling sorry for myself is a part of the job. In art there is always room to wallow (the kind I do anyway).

That is where art comes from. Art is something to do with all the feelings that would otherwise not do anything. Wallowing is not movement. Wallowing is stuck. Inertia. The art makes it move. Not go away but move.

I haven't seen anyone in days. My kid has been away for weeks. The keener got into a nationwide academic program. Got to take university classes ahead of grade 12 and she picked Vancouver. "Picked." I made her pick that one because June was out there and I was too afraid to let her go any old place all by herself.

When Willow first left, I relished the time. I wandered in and out of work, took walks, went to farmers' markets, saw friends.

After about a couple weeks, I stopped showering, only worked begrudgingly, started going through all the crap shows in Netflix's "Dramas with a Strong Female Lead." I had been living off cereal. Counting down days.

I am tired. I don't want to move. I watch the neighbours put on a second coat. The colour doesn't get any better.

June

This is my favourite place in this whole city. Happiest place on earth, I think. The breeze from the inlet smells of salt and summer. The sun hasn't yet burned away all the fog. Early. So early the dog beach is nearly empty. Just us and some young couple with a white terrier. This was a good idea.

I watch him play with our dogs. This man, my colleague, or former colleague now. I am not even going to fake name him. He is just *him*. Out in the sand, he gets right in there with my dog, his two, chasing and laughing. His goldens, Jess and Bess, are so much better trained than my two-year-old Lab, but they get along well enough. He throws a stick in the ocean and Zeke bounds through the water in arched jumps, high like a gazelle.

I am groggy from a shit sleep and anxious for what was coming but have a fresh paper-cupped americano in my hand and, Happiest Place on Earth hands down.

He comes up and sits on the log next to me. Too close. I inhale quick. Can smell his minty breath. That close.

"So, what kind of pretendian we dealing with then? Is this like the vague claims/grey area kind, or the jus' plain fakin' kind?" Like I said, we're well versed in dealing with these things.

I shrug, don't know why I keep doing that. "I can't find anything . . . it's just fake. I think." I keep saying that, but I know.

He breathes deep. "Is she involved with any of those 'Métis' organizations? Like the ones out east?"

I shake my head, again unsure. "Don't think so . . ."

"Has anyone claimed her? Like has she been adopted by anyone?"

"No," I say with certainty, for once. "She would have told me that. She would have told everyone that."

He sighs. "So for the past ten years, she's claiming a ridiculous, easily found to be untrue family story, and what has she gotten out of it?"

"Umm," I say slow, like I haven't made the list myself dozens of times over the last few hours, after long hours searching online and learning the specifics of the facts I tried to blur for so long. "A few grants designated for Indigenous artists, an award, a big award for Indigenous artists, her job—it's an Indigenous arts specialist that was earmarked for an Indigenous person. That's what I know."

"Yup, that's fraud," he says. "I'm sorry, June, that's messed up. That's your mom!"

"I know." My voice so quiet.

He doesn't say anything for a minute. A long moment we watch the dogs, the sun, a paddleboarder passing offshore playing hip-hop. The beats so clear even though they are far over the water.

"A statement is a good idea," he adds, finally. "Put it all out there. You could even post it yourself and get ahead of it." He dealt with a similar situation a few years ago when a writer claimed connection to his community.

I shake my head. Can't even pretend I could do that. "It's so . . . hard."

"I bet." There is coffee on his breath too, just a hint. "At least when it happened to us, we didn't know the fucker at all."

I shrug, again. Can't stop. I also suck in my gut.

"You could also say nothing. Lawyer up and stay quiet. I mean, it's family, it's different when it's family. No one would fault you if you wanted to stay out of it."

"But I . . . That feels like a cop-out." I didn't add that I've been copping out of this for so long. Too long.

"It's your mom. It's complicated when you love the person."

I don't explain that that isn't it. "If I did a statement, what should I say?"

He takes another breath and sits straighter. Is he sucking in his gut too? "Keep it simple and speak directly to the issue. You know your stuff. You know who you are." He looks at me way too long. "I mean, who thinks Métis just means mixed anymore anyway?"

Probably a lot of people, I don't say.

But it's like he heard. "How many times do we have to say it? That Métis actually means a whole people with a history, language, culture and years and years of struggle. These fakers don't get to have all that because of what, a family story? A spit test? 'Cause they, what, *feel* it's true? No. No way. None of that is what being Indigenous means, but of course, explaining all that becomes the work of actual Indigenous people. Again! Just adds to the emotional labour we already have to do. Don't take it on anymore, I say. Be concise. Get in, get out. Let them look up the rest."

I nod. Can't look at him. So many reasons. I smile. Think of something funny to say, end up with a lame "Good rant!"

"Think so? I think I kind of lost it in the middle there but you know, I try." He laughs and it's contagious. Warm.

The writer who claimed his community was absolutely eviscerated in the press, on socials, everywhere. His publisher pulled out of his contracts. He lost his teaching job and his appearances got publicly cancelled. He became a punchline seemingly overnight. He tried to sue everyone but it went nowhere as he had no proof anyone was lying. Quite the opposite, actually.

"I think my girls are gonna miss your little guy," he humours me as the better-behaved Jess nips at my puppy-school dropout.

I look over quick and smirk at him. Yes, he is too close. The heat of his arm against my nylon sleeve. I can't look too long. Instead, I watch the light grow, hit the buildings across the water in North Van. The windows sparkle like gems pressed into the side of the mountain.

"I'm going to miss having you around, Stranger." He nudges playfully. A performative friend gesture like a punch in the arm.

"Me too." I try to sound jovial but I am pretty sure it comes off sad. Or pathetic.

Zeke jumps back in the water, teasing the others with his big wet stick. Jess and Bess ignore him and wrestle each other. The terrier, now wet and dark with sand, and his humans leave.

I realize with a thud that this will be the last day. Our last day. Might never see him again. I look down at his hand considering, for a long time. Study his thumb, long fingers, nails, try to get the nerve to look up.

My phone startles me. Then I worry it could be Sigh. My dad. My sister. Whenever someone calls something is wrong.

I look. A Toronto number. Unknown. I groan. Back to annoyed. I switch it off.

"You got to get that?"

"Naw, just a robocall, I think."

"You sure?"

"Yeh, it's fine." But it's over. My nerve. That moment. The world flooded in and it was already gone.

lyn

Dad comes in talking. He's here all the time to fix stuff in my ever-breaking old house and retired now so talks long and slow. I don't want to tell him about the Renee stuff (totally making June do it) but he's in a talking mood so I don't even have to worry about it.

"His knee's not getting better he says. Was out all last season. Says he's going to be a lawyer now. Taking some SAT test." Dad settles into one of my kitchen chairs and I make a new pot of coffee. He's talking about my baby brother, Riel, who goes to school in Edmonton and up until recently also played hockey.

"The LSAT?" I say.

"Dunno."

"No, that's what it's called. The LSAT."

"Well I don't know."

"Well I'm telling you!"

"Whatever. He's taking some test. Don't know why he'd want to be a lawyer."

"Wasn't Aunty Margaret a lawyer?" Genuine question.

"She wishes. No, she wasn't but almost. She never made it. Now that's a story!"

Dad loves talking about my younger brother, his finally-a-son after three girls, but he loves telling family stories more. Especially the ones I know already but have to listen to again, like how my Great-Aunt Margaret was in law school but then beat up her boyfriend so got charged with assault and couldn't finish school and never got to be a lawyer (my family, I tell you). I let him say it all like I've never heard it before and make him a turkey sandwich.

"So, I guess it's good we get one lawyer." He doesn't notice me cringe. (We did have a lawyer, but they left me, Dad!) He goes on: "A lawyer and a doctor, how lucky am I?" (the doctor is my other baby sibling, Yoyo) and before I can react, he quickly adds: "And an artist and an academic and whatever brilliant thing your Willow is going to do. Yeh, I sure am lucky."

I give him a side-eye and ask, "You want chips or carrots?"

"Better have them baby carrots. Otherwise Kelly will give me grief. Always giving me grief, that one." (His wife.)

"Well, we all want you around as long as you can be, you know. Health and all that."

"Pretty sure Kelly just wants me to suffer but yeh, I'll be around for a while yet, I'm sure. Not that lucky."

I smile at his sarcasm. I have been raised to be a proper connoisseur of the stuff. It's our love language.

"You must be excited to have your girl home soon, hey? And your sister. I can't believe Juney's going to be living here. How long has it been?"

"She moved away two years before Willow was born, so what? Seventeen?"

"A whole teenager, almost an adult, ago. Bet you're going to be happy when she's around all the time, hey?"

"Betcha you are."

"A whole other old house to fix up. Lucky me."

"I think Sigh can handle himself."

"Good. He can fix yours then too."

"Like you'd let him."

"True, he probably won't know these old houses. They're cranky. At least your little sister had the sense to buy something new. You should sell this place and get one of those new condos. If you got a condo, I'd have nothing to fix."

"You'd miss me too much."

"Chance would be a fine thing." All gushy today.

I want to tell him. I think of telling him. But he's so happily fixing my sink and complaining. I clean up his plate and swear I can't find the words. (Hey Dad, your white ex-wife has been posing as an NDN to get all these awards and now getting outed as a pretendian and June is scared it'll fall back on us. More coffee?) I think it was all the explaining I'd have to do that stopped me. That and he kept going on about how great little Riel was at hockey and how they all thought he was destined for the NHL. Spent so much money on hockey things, camps, trainers.

"This will kill him, I think. You know one of those slow things that build up. He's talking all fine now but this has been his whole life, hey?"

"He'll be okay, Dad. He's made of tough stuff, that kid." And it was true, my too-tall baby brother, the world was his for the taking. And Dad was probably taking this harder than Riel anyway.

"Yeh, I do have pretty tough kids, hey?" He pops his head out from the cabinet to wink at me and wave his hand for me to pass him a tool. "Come by it honestly, you guys do."

"Yeh, I know." I smirk. "Must get it from Grandma."

June

I text with my niece again, check my bank app too many times to see if the money went through. I want to pack up my office and check off my to-do list. Don't want to think of unsent emails and situations I should really be dealing with.

The sky grows dark and cloudy again. Sigh makes dinner but I don't get up. The food sits on the counter untouched, and Zeke lies on the floor below never letting it out of his sight. Still, I rummage. I stack all the paperbacks, organize according to subject, theme, fiction, poetry. I always clean out and give away a few books every time we move. I accumulate a lot so need to thin them out every year or so. Try to limit myself. I only have two tall bookshelves but manage to wedge more on top of others, pile them on the floor, in the corners.

I consider a system of culling—maybe I should only take what I will need, but who knows what will come up. I think of what I have too much of and should take only what I really want, but they all give me joy and really, they are the only thing I hoard. It's for work, you see. I can always justify something if it's for work.

I can't give away poetry because print runs are so small. Have to keep all the ones I haven't yet read because I have to read them, obviously. Can't give away anything I might lend to a student or might fit on a syllabus. I sit in the middle of piles of books and can't think of a reason to let go of a single one. Not one.

I have tried, with Renee. I have spoken up.

A few years ago, when lyn freaked about it, and I saw the extent of it. What I thought was the extent of it. Renee's middle-aged white woman version of Woodland art and all the space she was genuinely trying to take up. Using her stupid alias to claim something that didn't belong to her. To pretend.

When I told her she shouldn't be doing that—she told me I didn't understand.

When I told her she is not Indigenous—she told me I was the one being silly.

When I told her all the wrong ways things like Shaman and Métis have been used, were still being used—she told me I should question what I was being taught. That I was learning from and working for the same institutions that have repressed "us" for so long. That I was the one who was colonized.

I started to get really worried about her, like something must be really wrong with her—she said she was fine and I shouldn't care so much about what people think. That I would understand when I was her age.

I probably should have done more but I was removed, or felt removed. I lived so far away. I stayed silent. I told myself if anyone asked, I would tell the truth. But no one asked so I didn't say anything.

I almost didn't take this job. I am the worst kind of activist. The inactive kind.

I should email the universities. My new one and my old one. The organizations I work with. I should prepare everyone for what's coming. I should actually do something for a change.

I get up, climb over my book piles, go to my desk and write. And rewrite and rewrite and rewrite and fix and edit, but can't press Send.

I save it to a draft, tell myself it's good to think about these things first, and let out a deep deep breath from down in my lower lungs. It's all the way dark now, and my book piles seem higher. Not one!

Sigh's asleep, stretched out across the couch, his legs so long they go over the arm. I pat my knee for Zeke to come, which he does in an instant and we go out. I want to go to the beach again. I don't want that last time to be the very last time we were there.

In the dark it's so different. The lights across the inlet as pretty as stars. Barges only shadows on the water. Zeke runs to the sand's edge, finds a stick and then a better one.

I sit on a log, not the same one.

lyn

Dad's told me the story so many times (but every time he thinks it's the first time) that when they first got together, Renee's mom (Mennonite) called my dad (brown guy) a "prairie n-word." To his face. Because she thought it was the actual name of what he was. That's what she said anyway. And she got away with it 'cause she was old.

Dad said Grandma (Renee's mom) actually said, "You look pretty put together for a prairie n-word. Clean. Well dressed." She said it with a nod like she was doing him a favour. An insult dressed like a compliment hidden deep within a slur. She wouldn't have thought he'd be offended. Not that he did anything or showed offence. Knowing Dad, he probably only nodded.

Once she heard, my Grandma Genie (Dad's mom) told everybody and none of my dad's family talked to any of Renee's family at their wedding. Grandma Genie thought the whole thing unseemly (the fact that the bride and groom were both teenagers didn't faze her) and never got over it. Still talks about it. No one insults her precious only child Jerome (that's what she called it, "insult").

When they were still together, Dad used to drive us out to visit Grandma (Renee's mom). Renee never learnt to drive so he'd take us all the way out there, then he'd roam the highways a couple hours and come pick us up at the allotted time.

He told me he was stopped by the RCMP more than once doing that, and one time we had to go get him from the detachment in Morden. I have no memory of it, but June said we drove over with Renee's brother (white guy) who was not convinced Dad was just minding his own business. He couldn't imagine why else they would pick him up.

After they split up, we didn't go out there much. Had to wait for Aunty Dell, the only one of Renee's siblings who lived in the city, to drive us. And it wasn't often. As Aunty Dell would say, "I can't do that to myself more than once or twice a year. The therapy alone costs too damn much. Never mind the wine."

I always thought it was weird she was so racist because Grandma had married a Frenchie (her word) and was considered pretty worldly for a Menno lady of her generation (Aunty Dell said that). Renee told us her parents moved out to a farm because her people never accepted him. Aunty Dell said Grandma just didn't want her sisters anywhere near her new exotic husband. Didn't let him go to town without her 'cause she was afraid he'd get off with someone.

I do remember this one time, Grandma was telling us that she was French now. Not Menno anymore. Because of who she married.

June had laughed before she realized Grandma was serious. "You're not French, Grandma. You're still Mennonite even if you married a French person."

"You don't know what you're talking about. My last name is French now. That means I'm French."

"That's just your married name, Grandma. It doesn't mean you're French."

"Well my kids are French. So I am too."

"They're Mennonite too. You're Mennonite."

"You can't be two things, Juniper. You can only be one thing."

"That's not true. We're Métis and we're Mennonite and we're French. All together."

"Don't say that. Don't you even say that. You're a pretty girl. A beautiful girl. Don't let anyone tell you different."

"I know, Grandma . . ."

"You don't have to say that. You're white because your mother is white. End of story."

"It doesn't work that way, Grandma."

"Sure it does. No one would even know to look at you. Just stay out of the sun and you'll be fine."

I didn't say anything. I never said anything when I was a little kid. Especially not out there.

June

Every time we move I think this time, this time! I will really do it. I will give away some books. Pass along a few others. Keep only what I need. Let them the fuck go. But I never do. I need all of them. They each have some piece, some thought, some thing I want to take with me. This time like all the other times, I am going to pack them up, cart them across a great distance, keep them with me. Don't let go.

I turn to my filing cabinet. Piles of papers I should have recycled years ago. I scan the titles, the topics, the reading lists. I want to know and remember whatever they can tell me about myself.

I've always known who I am but didn't always think being Michif was enough. I think we were lucky to grow up knowing our culture, our family's story, but Dad wouldn't have called it lucky. He would explain it like, "Those who passed for white passed for white, but we were too dark, so no choice there."

His Grandpa Mac taught him to be proud of who he was, and he grew up knowing the stories of resistance, kinship, solidarity and passed them to us. I wrote a paper on Louis Riel when I was in junior high. My history teacher asked me what book I got it all from and I said, way too sure of myself, "My dad!"

She called it "fanciful" and made me rewrite it using only the books in the library. I knew they were wrong. Dad even said so, but he also said just do the work and not complain or get into any trouble. That I could show them by doing good work. Getting good grades. So I did. Rewrote it and got an A+. Stuck to the "facts" and wrote between the lines. The teacher didn't even notice the two versions were basically the same, only different in tone, really.

I have stacks of papers from my undergrad. Back when I printed them up and put them in manila envelopes. Got them back red marked and commented upon. The look of them, the smell of ink, makes me nostalgic for something I completely forgot about.

I flip through my tattered books, the ones I've carried with me for decades. Smile at the pencilled comments I made in the margins. Back when I thought I knew it all. Before I knew better.

My dissertation was about Michif women in literature. What they write about, why they write. It was great actually. I got to interview all my heroes, Lee Maracle, Marilyn Dumont, Maria Campbell, Beatrice Culleton Mosionier, and wrote their words among my own.

At its heart it's about the catharsis and power of lifewriting, and how these trailblazers used their own stories to not only heal themselves but through their art also healed those of us who saw ourselves in their words. How that empowerment fuels the revolution. The personal becomes political because it shines light on colonial oppression, reflects the colonial gaze back onto itself.

Inevitably, the content of their words, like the content of many of our lives, is filled with trauma and the intergenerational effects of constant, ever-changing genocides, but still, theirs are mostly stories about strength. Their strength as individuals, what they have and what they give out. Their people's strength. Our people.

It wasn't a bad dissertation, though not publishable as it was, I know that, and it was 2010, the TRC had just begun, Idle No More was a few years yet. My advisors had to include a chair of a Native Studies department—this old white guy I will not name—he was the one who said to my face that my work was too emotional to truly interrogate the subject, that true scholarship required objectivity. I should have walked out. I felt like walking out. Well actually I felt like crying but that seemed to only prove his point. Tears did well up in my eyes. Someone told someone else about this, and I became the one who cried while defending my dissertation.

I was furious with myself. Hated that I couldn't keep it in. Didn't fault that jackass for a long time.

There were two Native Studies jobs opening when I finished. I didn't get either one. Both candidates were dudes. One white.

One of my other advisors, a Nehiyaw scholar who was outspoken by the standards of the time, told me later that she wanted to say something too, but stayed silent. We both did. Both felt we had to. That was the worst part. We didn't think we'd survive reacting. She helped me get my post-doc in Brisbane. She told me I should explore Indigenous nations globally and keep writing about the women. So that's what I did. I have ever since. Silent and taking it everywhere except in the work.

In Winnipeg I am going to study Michif women from earliest records and stories to present. I am going to dig into Sarah Ballenden, Annie Bannatyne, Maria Thomas, Mary Sally Mactavish. Through biography, I will show how the work of Indigenous women made and continues to make our culture and this place as a whole. How the matriarchy continues.

I want to go to Edinburgh and learn about all their ties and relations over there. I want to weave their stories into the larger narrative of all matriarchal societies, forever crushed down by colonization and white supremacy yet still holding everything together. How abusing and silencing women coincides with pillaging of Mother Earth. How lifestories are still so integral to the revolution because they empower all of us, lighting up all the dark places.

I want to continue to write about Michif history and politics but also about this trauma we carry, how it's everywhere and in everyone and manifests in so many different ways, and is in some ways just another something to overcome and heal from. How the work of the Other is never ever done because the oppressor finds new ways to burden us. How we all simultaneously heal and also guide each other to healing.

But that's all dreams and what that jackass would have called "bad scholarship." I am going to document cool women stories for the university to make record of, historical figures we need to know more about. I am going to incorporate new voices, older voices, and frame the narrative around power and the reclamation of stories and agency. I want to write about how we overcome, how we go forward, how we get to joy, together.

Something like that. I am not sure exactly what it will be in the end. The one thing I am sure of is it's going to be really really fucking emotional all the way through.

lyn

Shannon just had a baby. Shannon left me and got married right away, and then—baby. Right away. They must have been expecting in the wedding photos. They both wore white. It was beautiful. I looked and looked at every single picture when they posted them. Returned to them often. Cried over them. Often. Examining every detail. Trying to see the truth the knowing the *when* in their smiles. They looked so happy.

Only glanced at the baby photos though. His name a name they said they liked once, one I didn't (stupid name).

> I might be a mess but I've done it all
> DBT CBT IFS EFT EMDR ACT talk therapy
> (of course)
> Elders Teachers Ceremony yoga somatics
> witchcraft spells ritual
> Buddhism meditation prayer music music art
> art art

Before I thought better of it, I messaged them a quick Congrats and looked away. I DMed without thinking, without considering that it didn't need to be a private conversation. Out of habit

Their profile pic their wife and them. One of the wedding photos.
Not the best one.

> I believe in everything or maybe I
> believe in anything I have
> searched for joy searched for peace love balance
> compassion not happiness will settle for
> contentment I have
> had my moments

The thread above my Congrats included every single message
we've ever sent on there. Years of them. I've scrolled back before.
All the way to the beginning. Read our relationship in reverse.
Then the way it went again.

I liked it better in reverse.

> vicarious trauma institutional trauma trauma
> from racism trauma from sexism childhood
> trauma attachment trauma abandonment trauma
> abandonment wound core wound codependency
> I've read them all

> had them all?

I was halfway through our first breakup when they messaged
back and the thread fast-forwarded over the years I had just gone
over to their
"thanks" smiley face. Friendly.
Relieved

I went back up through the breakups the fights the love shared
photos funny GIFs all the way to the beginning and stayed there
stayed up too late,
cried too much thought too many
thoughts.

There were also sad songs.
I sat out on my deck with only
a long summer sky to stare at
to implore for
answers.

      in the end

      all this
      work has amounted to
      brief
      reprieves in the relentless
      beating
      my
      self
      up

Friend Request Accepted. You and Shannon are now Friends.

   hey
   Hey yourself!
   how you doing?
   Better now that I'm talking to you ...

tiny moments I might just convince
myself I actually do
want to
save
my own
life

I wish this Renee stuff would stop already, but I know better.
What I actually want to go away never does.

3

weathering

June

I take Willow to our new favourite diner for lunch and then walk to the bunny beach. This was our first outing when she came out at the beginning of summer, and she wanted to go again before she left. The sun is out and the wild bunnies are hoping around like they own the place, which of course, they do.

I tell her a sanitized version of what's going on. She knew some. More than I thought she would. I guess lyn told her back when it all started. For some reason, that surprises me.

"I can't believe all this is happening. Why would Crazy Grandma dig her heels in like that? It's really unhinged." Her fading blue hair flopping like a limp mohawk. Her eyes a hazel version of my sister's dark ones.

"You shouldn't call her that."

"What?"

"Crazy."

"You do."

"I shouldn't either."

"Seems to be shoe-fitting type thing."

We get ice cream and walk along the water. I find it odd to walk without my dog. Always think I'm forgetting something.

It's getting cold here. Cold already.

Willow: "You all packed up?"

"Not at all. I've been too busy with this stuff."

"That's too bad. You should be enjoying this. Last days here. I love it here. And you got so many things to look forward to—your big fancy job, new house. It's exciting!" She's always been like this. Willow was born an old lady. A mom.

"I am. Well, I think I am. The house and job are going to be so much work though."

"But it'll be neat. Having you home. I'm excited."

A thud of guilt in my gut. I moved away before she was even born. Have always felt like I was never around enough. Our relationship has grown only in intense spurts of visits, then long hauls of absence. This summer is the most I've ever seen and known her, and she's almost grown. "So you like it here, hey?"

"Oh for sure. I am going to apply everywhere—Simon Fraser, UVic. I don't want to stay in Winnipeg for anything."

"I was the same."

"And you got to live in so many amazing places! I want to do that. I want to go everywhere. What was your favourite?"

"Um, probably Aotearoa. Wellington or Rotorua. It's beautiful down there."

"I can't wait. I'd love to take a gap year and travel but pretty sure lyn would flip."

"She would."

Willow nods as if thinking on this.

I give her a sly smile. "You could always do it anyway."

At her very detailed direction, I take pictures of her walking along the path. Long vids of her looking contemplative in the light that she says she'll edit down later. I try not to giggle at her serious face. She looks like a baby. She is a baby.

We sit on a bench and I show her my statement. The email not sent. She makes some word change suggestions but says I did a good job.

"Gee thanks, Mom," I joke, then, "I am so nervous about it."

"Why? You're only speaking your truth. No one can mess with your truth."

"Sounds like something *she* said."

"Crazy Grandma?"

I give her a look.

She only smiles and gets away with everything. "Racial identity isn't only about you, it's about community," she says. "Who you claim but also who claims you, right."

"You sound like someone who's just taken their first university course."

"True story."

"It's so hard for me to talk to her. Easier to write emails to other people."

"Oh, you're so avoidant. lyn is the same. Pure ostriches."

I'm about to ask.

"Heads in the sand."

"Ah."

"You gotta separate the two things. One is your family relationship with this person, that's one thing. The other is your professional self, your public self, your brand. Your brand can't be quiet. That's not who you are."

I put my phone away. This old soul with a baby face putting me to shame. "When did you get so smart?"

"Pssh, lyn's had me in therapy since I could talk. This stuff's easy. Now can you get me over there by those rocks? Before we lose this light?"

lyn

I shouldn't've answered. I never answer unknown numbers. But it was Toronto and I sometimes get work out of Toronto and:

"Hello, I'm looking for lynden stranger?"

"Speaking."

"Hi, Ms. stranger. I am calling from the Globe and—"

"What?! Crap. How did you get this number?"

"I'm writing a story about the artist known as Raven Bearclaw, your mother?"

"Raven Bearclaw is a made-up name. Anyone with any sense would know that."

"Yes, her legal name is Renee Stranger and that's your mother, right?"

I stammer. Think about hanging up (should have hung up). "I haven't talked or had anything to do with her in a long time. Years!"

"But she's still your mother. Your biological mother, is that right? Did you know her claims of Indigenous ancestry are being questioned?"

"I don't know anything about her or her 'claims.' She's white. That's all I know." I think I'm sweating (was totally sweating).

"Are you reluctant to speak because her tenuous claims would put your claims into question as well? You claim Indigenous ancestry too, don't you?"

"What? What are you talking about? We're Métis . . . Michif on my dad's side."

"Can you prove that?"

"Um yeh. Of course."

"You don't sound sure."

I literally stuttered. "I am unsure about everything to do with this . . . conversation. Raven Bearclaw is the most made-up name, like couldn't any of you see that before?" (Have I mentioned I don't do well with conflict?)

"You didn't answer my question."

My eyes shoot around my studio, trying to focus on something. Anything. Outside a crow caws. "What are you even talking about?" (Even the crow had a better comeback.)

"Are you afraid to answer the question, Ms. stranger?"

I think I made a sort of sputtering noise.

He laughed and not in the good way. "Can I quote you on that?"

"Quote this." I finally do hang up (meaning the quote was the hang-up. Even though it was just a beep really and rather anticlimactic).

I stomp upstairs vibrating with anger. Sick with it. Pace a circle on my kitchen floor trying to calm down. Not calming down. I go out to the deck, the warm sun. To hell with the clouds. Fuck the fucking moment.

June

She was out of breath. It takes me a minute to figure out what she's saying. Was walking Zeke. Turn down a quiet street so I can hear her better.

"Sounds like the same reporter, hey? What did you say?"

"Nothing. He was all 'her claims' and then he said something like 'your claims' and then I said 'like hell.'" She sounds like she's walking too.

I stop though. "Really? That's what you said? The article will quote you as saying 'Like hell.'"

"Naw. I actually said that our Métis 'claims' come from our dad."

"Okay, that's not bad. That's the truth so that's not bad." Zeke whines so I pick up the pace again.

"And that she's the fakest NDN in all of fake NDN town."

"That's not good!"

"Whatever. He's not going to quote me. We weren't quoting."

"I don't know if that's how it works, lyn."

"I'm not worried about it." Stubborn.

"I wonder if I should call him. I should write him something. Make this statement . . ."

"So you're going to fancy professor say 'she's the fakest NDN in all of fake NDN town'?"

"Something like that." I stop at a tree. Or rather Zeke does.

"You're really worried, hey? Now I might be worried. This is real." She's not really worried. Just saying that to make me feel better. She seems to stop though. Or sit. Her voice calmer.

"It is. I think it'll be big. It'll be one of the big ones."

"A couple years ago, I really wanted this to happen." Vulnerable.

"What changed?"

"I don't know if anything changed, I just, I think I accepted nothing was going to happen and now that it is . . ."

"You feel guilty?"

"No! Why would I feel guilty? That's so stupid and . . ."

"Unfair?"

"Maybe."

"It is all stupid and unfair. All of it."

"It's not on us, June. It has nothing to do with us." Firm.

"I wish you were right."

"I am right. I'm so right. You should just keep that in your head as a given and we'd save so much time." She's back to sarcasm so must be feeling better.

I laugh. Let her hear me laugh.

She sighs. "Yeh. We should really tell Dad."

We should.

lyn

Midday texts:

Grandma Genie—come get this pickerel alredy

Aunty Dell—did that reporter call you too?

Willow—[happy dog compilation, followed with] 2 more sleeps!!!!!!

Yoyo—Let's have pizza tonight. I need to get out of my house.
(Totally heard what's happening. From Willow or June. Someone should really tell Dad.)

This clay is from the earth. This specific batch from the Seine
River, pulled in early spring at a favourite place. Where I get
most of my clay. Where my people have lived for generations. I
have been working my way through it all summer. It's rocky, so
I spend a lot of time sifting through the wet, picking out tiny
stones, grains of glass, anything that would cause cracks or
breaks when I fire. The shells and stones and bones I use to
smooth are from there, too. All from the same home. All together

63

here with me. I use too much water. I have been told this so many times. But there's a chafing to the dryness and I prefer the smooth of the wet.

I started this whole project by making too many of these little pots. Was selling the ones that look good. The ones I could cook and paint. I paint flowers mostly. In the style of floral beadwork that looks like smeared dots. They sell quickly because I am lucky.

The other ones, the ones with what others would call faults or mistakes but I call personality, I started to collect. For no reason at first. For my project now. I have dozens of these offcut type vessels. I don't know yet where they will live or what they will do or if I will even show anyone. I only want to keep them. I look at them all on the shelves and know I should soak some and reuse the clay but I can't seem to. They all have something—a lean, a crack, a wavy line that was supposed to be straight. I think I make them off on purpose. Like them better that way.

Don't know what it will all be, but know when I do, they will be together. Maybe I can make a pattern, make them make sense. I think they will make sense if I put them all together and look.

I'm doing this with a lot of things, it seems.

With everything

Hunched over at the table, arms working. I move my hands with knuckle cracks and massages. I use warm water so they can keep moving when they get cold. My body focused my mind wanders roams a whole journey every day.

Art used to make me heal. Or at least felt like it did or else I wouldn't've kept doing it. I started to make art to fix myself, and it did save my life, countless times. Or I thought it did. That's when I didn't know what I was doing, just did it for fun. I'd paint, write, draw, play in the mud, anything that made me feel better. I didn't think about what I was doing. I'd be like a kid. Well, I was a kid but would act even younger. Be the kid I was before I learnt about the other things, before I was ruined. I did art like I was four years old. Played like no one was watching.

Art is only healing when you think no one is watching. Once you do it for other people it ceases to be yours. It becomes theirs. For them.

That's okay. It's a giving. It's a gift to the world and for their healing. But you, the artist, you are then the healer, not the healed.

That's some bullshit right there, but sometimes it's true.

June

I stare at all my stuff, scattered on the floor, and contemplate my next move. Try to see everything in front of me, how it might go, what might happen, all the many possibilities.

I rewrite the statement, again, and paste it in an email to the reporter. Then I do the same with a quick explanation on top and address it to the university I am going to work at, the one I used to work at and a couple organizations I am involved with. I look at them all, one after the other, in my Drafts folder. A tidy list. In order. Saved. I also paste one in Notes for my socials but don't post. I vow to put it up as soon as the article comes out. I should schedule it. I don't.

I check my socials. I check everything. Look for hints of it. Nothing yet.

What I really want to do is message him. Should give him the new version of my statement and ask for his opinion. He would think of all the angles too, and know, and make me feel better. But I can't call him. I can only think of his hand there, on his lap, on the log at the beach, his thumb.

Once when I first got to the city, we went for coffee. He got a call from some reporter asking him to quote on something. And right there I watched him turn it on. His face serious, his voice even. So concise. So perfect.

I have always wanted to have perfect words.

When he got off the phone, I said, "Impressive."

"Oh that." Not just coy, genuinely like it was nothing. "Well, I'm glad to have impressed you." His smile turned sly, playful.

So dangerous.

lyn

When my parents split up for good, June stayed with Dad and I went with Renee. I don't remember it being a choice.

She couldn't afford much so she had to get a small place, but it was close to my school and had an elevator. Loved that elevator.

"You fight with your sister all the time anyway," Renee told me as we organized the bedroom closet. "This way you'll miss her."

We were going to share the room. I got half of the closet for my hanging things and my little dresser tucked underneath. There was another bedroom but she needed that for her studio. She was learning the guitar. "You always want to sleep with me anyway."

She seemed so happy those first weeks. I was excited to have special time only with her. It wasn't bad. Unless her boyfriend came over and then I'd have to sleep on the couch. I would cuddle up with blankets Grandma Genie knitted and sometimes keep the TV on quiet long after Renee told me to turn it off and go to sleep.

All my other stuff went into and stayed in boxes in corners—
toy box, Barbie box, special box—they were pretty enough, I
decorated them myself with markers and sparkles and glued
things, but they were still boxes, placed out of the way, set
aside. Decorated.

But we were good for a while.

Those first weeks, she'd tell me:

"You're my special girl. You and I are just the same. I love
June, of course, but you're my special one."

"I'm sad she's not here too but at least I have you."

"I'm so glad you're here. I don't know what I'd do without
you."

"I need you, lynnie lyn, you make me feel better."

June and I would hang out at either home on weekends. My
sister became someone I had sleepovers with, her house or mine.
We were considered old enough to be on our own after school,
so we'd call each other then, when we were alone in our separate
homes. We weren't even that far away, could walk to each other,
but we mostly stayed where they put us, like children do.
Trusting, even after we know better.

I remember being alone a lot. Hating when Renee's boyfriend
ShitFace was around which was always. But then hating when he
left too because Renee would be in her (our but really her) room.
Like she shut off when he wasn't around. Like she didn't func-
tion unless she had him.

After about a year, she got a residency in Bali and took off. Didn't tell me. Dad did. He picked me up from school one day with our apartment key and told me to pack up my stuff.

Luckily it was still in boxes.

June

I had met him in Sydney. The colleague. Sigh and I went to Australia on a whim after my visa expired in Aotearoa, but I couldn't get work. Didn't want to leave but couldn't get a job in a coffee shop. He had come in for a conference I went to. Spoke about bodily sovereignty and safety, about dismantling the system and Indigenizing the rebuild. One of those speakers who looks directly at you and you swear they are talking just to you.

I went up to him afterwards. Waited in line behind all the other fangirls. I thought up an intelligent question I have since forgotten. He smiled deeply.

"Thank you thank you," he said in his language. "Where are you from?"

"Winnipeg." I said. And didn't have to explain where Winnipeg was for the first time in years.

"Ah geez, Winipek. What are you doing down here?"

"Writing. Trying to write. Just finished a post-doc not too long ago." It had been a few years but he didn't need to know that.

"What institutes do you work with? I'd love to hear about your work."

I blathered words together. "Oh I was at UQ for a while then lecturing at U OF A—Auckland—but I came up here to just well,

write." Didn't add that my husband was working here, support-
ing my slacker ass with his hard labour. Didn't even add I had one.

"Nice place to do that. You should be teaching though."

I nodded. Probably waited too long to say anything.

"And you should come home. We need young people like you
up there."

It felt like a calling. A beacon. For a second anyway. For a second,
I would have gone wherever he asked me to go. We had been away
close to five years then. I felt adrift. Was running out of options.

For years my work had risen up up up all supposedly amounting
to something but then it was nothing. I was plateaued if not
slumped, spending my days walking around the beaches, hiking
along the ocean, feeling the hot hot sun. Not writing.

He said he knew of a lecturer position in Van. Would put in a
good word. Send an email.

Sigh was more than willing to go home. "We've been away long
enough," he said and it felt so final. Our wandering youth was at
its end. I thought it was our life but it was only a phase.

I got the job. I messaged him right away and he said he wasn't
surprised. That I deserved it. It was a lecturer, term, small
school. Didn't really want it but once I had it, couldn't say no.

It wasn't an intelligent question and I have never forgotten. I
literally said: "I like what you said." Pretty sure there was a giggle
in there, too.

lyn

Yoyo comes over, two hours late. She holds a bottle of wine in each hand. "Can we order food like now? I am starved."

"Who told you?"

"Told me what?" She arches her brow (always been her tell).

I roll my eyes and start looking up food options.

"I just wanted to get out of the house. Matt's sick of me. Or I'm sick of him, maybe. He's just gonna play his little video games all night. Won't even notice I'm not there."

"Ah, romance."

"I tell you, this adulting. So fucking boring. If I have to have one more conversation about hydro prices or how we should do the sidewalk—stones or concrete—I am going to lose it. It's all so, dull, hey?"

"You love it."

"Yeh. I do. Some of it. We painted too. Hate painting. But love picking out colours."

"That's the artist in you."

"Yeh and I got no art left otherwise. Too much adulting. I am literally studying all day and night. I study so much I don't have time to eat. Literally studying my ass off . . ."

She turns to show me her not even thirty-year-old arse.

I scoff. "Like you had one to begin with, bannock bum."

"Fuck off just because you have one of those Menno round asses everyone wants."

"Why are you checking out my arse?"

"You wish." She shrugs and plops down on her nonexistent ass. "You won't believe the shit that happened to me in lab . . ." She always starts by complaining, this one. It's like she wants to make sure I know she suffers too. Or she's apologizing for how good she has it. It's annoying. I am annoyed.

By the end of the second bottle of wine she'll be crying about one of her teachers who told her how good she was doing, or telling me how Matt makes her pancakes and fixes her computer, "like every time, no matter, no matter what is wrong. He just knows!"

Then she'll pass out on the couch. She plans to sleep up in Willow's room but doesn't make it to the stairs.

I will cover her with another blanket Grandma Genie knitted for me that I've had for years. My baby sister will moan, turn over and snore like she did even when she was a little kid. And I will fill with love for her. I do love her so much.

She was born right before Renee went to Bali (yes, only a year after they split). I barely knew Kelly, her mom, 'cause I was hardly there at first. And if I was, I wouldn't talk to her unless I had to. Didn't even acknowledge the baby stuff. In the few pictures of me at the time, I am sulking. June made fun of it all behind their backs but still was nice to Kelly, nicer than I thought she should be.

I remember thinking I didn't care. Or not wanting to. I remember Renee making some snide comments about it all, sitting on the couch telling ShitFace, "Don't know why that young girl is jumping into this so quick. It's not like he has any money. Guess she's not used to much. Sounds like she's trying to trap him, if you ask me."

I was at the kitchen table trying to do my math homework. Trying to listen to my Discman too loud but it kept stopping. My Pearl Jam CD had a skip in the middle of "I Am Mine" but I would play it up to that point every time just in case one day it would work.

"He's rushing into things way too quick. Trying to prove something by the looks of it."

I went over there when Yoyo was a few days old. June was holding her and I was suddenly rigid with jealousy. Thinking of this little baby taking even my sister away from me.

Dad came up and hugged me so hard. "I'm so glad you're here, lynnie. I am so lucky with all these girls, hey? So lucky." He didn't cry but it was the closest I'd ever seen him.

He ordered pizza and we talked and laughed all night. Eventually Kelly just put the baby in my arms. I had been looking in the other direction. Really didn't want her to but, then there was this person.

This perfect little person was there with the weight of her across my bent elbows, warming my chest. She looked at me. I swear she looked up like she loved me. Like I was the one with the answers who could tell her, show her, lead. I was her big sister. Her June.

And that was me, hooked.

June

I remember one time, early on in our relationship, Sigh had a fight with his mom.

They'd been talking on the phone. They have a text thread now, him, his mom and sisters, and they talk every day. Every damn day. But this was back when he had to call her. I remember we were in Brisbane, had just got there, like still didn't have two forks or anything. I was sitting on the futon that was our bed and couch when he came in the room, raging. They'd been yelling. She was telling him how he was wasting his life following me around the world and he should come home and work with his brother-in-law. A common rant she had that eventually came true. But that first time, Sigh was livid. It takes a lot to get him going and he had never shown the slightest annoyance at his mother before this.

I remember watching him and preparing myself in my body, in my head. Saying it was okay and some families just don't talk to each other, and I know what it's like so I can support him. I was thinking of how best to support him through this.

The next day he was laughing on the phone with her, a group call with one of his sisters, his very young nephew on the line too.

When he got off, I said, carefully, just in case: "Are you okay? I thought you were mad at her."

"She doesn't give a shit if I'm mad at her. She calls anyway."

"Was she mad?"

"No, she didn't even talk about it. Stuff like that doesn't bother us."

"Stuff like what?"

"I dunno, fights, disagreements."

"Ohhh," I said long like a breath. "Normal. Weird."

It's not like I was totally clued out. Dad and Kelly are pretty normal. Annoying and basic, but normal. I don't remember having a fight with them in my adult life. They've never gotten mad at me for not visiting or asked me to support them publicly. They've never asked me to bail them out of something they got themselves into. They never had to. They wouldn't do that. They wouldn't even know how.

lyn

I knew Aunty Dell would still be up. She stays up late like me.
Even later, I think. Most nights she's the last one to make a play
on our game before sleep.

"Whoa an actual phone call! Did someone die?"

"No. Just wanted to call." I stared out at the night sky. "All
this stuff."

"Ah, so just the death of dignity."

"That reporter called you too?"

"Oh yah. Serves me right for being listed."

"What did you say?"

"The truth. Too old to remember any lies."

"Yikes."

"Well, she should've known better. Crazy lady. What the hell
was she thinking?"

"I don't know, Aunty. I don't know." I hear her exhale a cig-
arette, rummage around with something. Fidgeting. "Are you
okay, Aunty?"

"Oh you know me. I'm always okay. I mean, I'm worried
about her. I'm angry at her but still, I've seen how these things
go and she's still my sister. Stubborn fool that she is."

"Did you talk to her?"

"Naw, she wouldn't take my calls. Hasn't for years. Who knows where she is or who she's with, even. None of us have heard from her in a while."

"That's sad."

"Yah, it is. I'm sad for her. I am sad for the people who she's hurt with all this. What it's doing to you girls, and everyone. Not right. Not who we were raised to be at all. Real glad my mom didn't live to see all this." It was the first time her voice sounded old. Or I heard it as old.

"You should come over for supper. Willow and June will be here soon. You should come visit. See June's new house."

"As long as you're not cooking." She laughs one of her smoker's laughs. "No, that'd be nice. Sometime soon."

She gave another long exhale and we sat in the comfortable silence and the night awhile.

June

Sigh packs up the bedroom while I finally cram my books in the too-big boxes, then wrap them with too much tape, as if that would make up for how incredibly heavy they are.

"How's it going in here?" Sigh carefully places his crate of collectables. Special-made crate. Special collectables. Custom-made glass shelf. They're fucking toys.

"Are you taking all those? I thought you were going to sell some?"

"I only got two of these. You have five boxes of books already." Points.

"This is my job. I need these things to work."

"You have four copies of *Halfbreed*!"

"They're different editions!"

"Pfft." He walks off

"Pfffft." I am louder. "This one even has *a new chapter*!"

But he's back in the bedroom, pretending he can't hear me.

He comes back out with the second crate. "You should stop and eat."

"I still haven't done the kitchen."

"I can do that."

"You have never done that." I should be nicer to him. It's not his fault I'm so stressed.

"Everything's going to be okay, you know."

I stop. The way he cuts through, sees me, still jars me open. I don't cry. So sick of crying. I'm mad now. I wish I was mad all the way through.

"I feel so useless. It's like if I could only say the right thing, then she would listen."

"It's not on you. Besides, she seems like she's too far down the rabbit hole to hear sense, even if you knew the *perfect* thing to say."

"I know, but something." I rub my eyes. My face. "I mean I told her. I bet people have been telling her for years."

"Who knows? She got these awards, these what, accolades. Who wouldn't want that?"

"I know but, it's not. I just don't get that thinking. I mean I can't get over my imposter syndrome in . . . anywhere. I always think I'm a fraud. That people will see through me and know I'm full of shit."

"Because of this?"

"No. Well, this has made it worse, yeh, but that's how I've always felt, you know. I'm just a stupid kid from Winnipeg and have no business being a professor doing professor things. And then she just goes in, confident in her fake authority, and takes it all? I don't get it."

"She didn't just take it. Someone gave it to her. That's the problem. You taught me that."

"But why? Why are they still doing that? Treating culture like a box to check, like something they can get. Only accepting the most palatable, most white version of us and then selling these frauds back to us."

"Capitalists, man. Motherfuckers."

He always makes me laugh. Not a wear-me-down laugh like lyn does, but really laugh.

"I'm just so . . . afraid."

"Of what? You know who you are, as you always tell me."

"Do I? What do I really know?" There is a world where all of this is upside down, where Renee is sensible and I'm insane. Sometimes I think I'm really living in that one.

"You know you're Métis. Your dad is Métis. Your family has lived that experience and know who they are."

"And I've always felt so lucky with that. That we've always, no matter what we've faced, been . . . proud? Not proud. I mean *I'm* proud. Now. But I don't know that they were always proud. My dad, his family, faced so much bullshit, so I don't know they would say 'proud.' Or could anyway."

"The world tells you it's a horrible thing, eventually you start believing it."

"Or acting like you do. To get by."

"Did I ever tell you when we were growing up out here, everyone thought we were Asian and Mom never corrected them?"

"Yeh, you've told me that."

"It's kind of sad that, hey."

"Yeh, it's sad. As I've said the millions of times you've told me before."

"You're cranky."

"I'm sorry." I sigh from my gut. As deep as I can. I should be so much nicer to him. "There's so much to get over. So many ways we've been cheated out of being ourselves."

Tired again. I want to curl up in the dark. Stop. Everything. Still have the kitchen to do.

Reading my mind, or seeing my wandering eyes, my love says: "I am going to take Zeke for a run, get Willow, and we'll pick up lunch. Then we will help you with whatever's left and we'll have the child labour to help load the trailer. We'll get it all done, don't worry."

He kisses the top of my head. Full of love.

"Tomorrow," I say with a sigh.

"Tomorrow!" Sigh says. He smiles though.

lyn

Renee came home from Bali after only a few weeks. When she came to Dad's she said she quit because she missed us so much (got kicked out) and that she got a new bigger apartment (evicted) with her new (old) boyfriend ShitFace and that I should get my stuff and come.

June told me to stay. Dad said it was my decision. Yoyo cooed up at me from her blanket spread out on the floor. Kelly disappeared into the house. Renee said nothing but looked all sad and refused to look at the baby, I remember that, so I tried to look excited for her. Because she looked sad. There was a whole room for me at least (glorified closet).

I packed a bag quick and left without saying goodbye to the baby. Felt bad about that for a long time. My sister had her arms crossed in front of her chest and told me to call her as soon as I got there. (Didn't do that either.)

I truly hated ShitFace. He didn't care about me in the slightest and pretty sure he never even bothered to learn June's name. I only cared about him because when he was there, Renee flitted about him like a moth to a light, like a mother to a child, and when he wasn't, she was sleeping.

Once we were living with him, he was always there, smoking his Export As on the couch, sipping Club beer, and she was happy. He didn't talk to me that much, only every now and then when he had to tell me what was wrong with me.

"You're really fucking miserable, aren't you?" It was a Saturday. I wanted to watch cartoons but he had the remote.

Renee had laughed like it was a joke. "She really is. Aren't you, hun? Can't you smile, lynnie? Give us a smile."

I should've given her the finger.

After that, Miserable became my nickname. Miserable was their term of endearment. Miserable was what I became.

I leant into it. I stretched moods out for days. I gave scoffing and humphing flare. I could roll my eyes so hard I made myself dizzy.

It only took a few months before he stormed out with a packed bag. They had been fighting in their room so I got to watch my show. Then he slammed the door so hard things on the shelf shook. She turned to me and screamed. "Why can't you just be happy for a change?! Be nice to him?!"

The bedroom door slammed. Not as hard.

The sitcom laugh track followed.

I had been doing my homework at the coffee table. Watching *Friends*.

But that wasn't the end (I should be so lucky). ShitFace came back. I remember apologizing, seemingly for existing. I remember spending the summer mostly at Dad's. Riel was a baby then, Yoyo a crazy toddler, and Dad and Kelly were always busy with them. June was obsessed with school but would actually pay attention to me in the summer so that's probably why I stayed. Probably also why I went back to Renee's in the fall.

The time in between ShitFace's comings and goings got shorter and shorter, but the cycle was the same. For years (three) he would appear smoke on the couch drink Club. Renee would giggle and wear makeup. She'd cook food. Whole suppers, dessert and everything. She'd practise her guitar and write songs. Beautiful melodies. She'd be an artist. Be fun. Laugh. Walk me to school even. The fighting would start in the evening. The crying would wake me up in the night. No one would get up and make sure I got to school.

When the whole thing came and went in a day, I went to Dad's. I thought for good. I wanted it be anyway. Renee showed up after a week and I thought it was to get me.

"I got a place in Turks and Caicos! That's the Caribbean. It's such a prestigious residency. A whole year!"

I imagined myself on the beach, getting a tan. In my mind my school would be right beside the ocean.

She left on a Thursday.

She *was* gone for a whole year.

June

I should've kept going. No, I should have taken a break, meditated or taken a bath, gone for a run, something soothing. I finished my office. Wanted to feel a sense of accomplishment. But in the quiet after the hurry, everything that just ebbed flowed right the fuck back.

I tried to breathe, tried to dive into the millions of things to do. Texted Willow that Sigh was on his way, in case he forgot to, which of course he fucking did. Then the landlord to confirm the walk-through. I didn't want to call my sister. Or maybe I should have been clear: I wanted her to comfort me, not make me comfort her.

"When are you going to be on the road?"

"Getting up at five because—"

She says it with me: "*Road trips start first thing*." This is something Dad drilled into us very early in life.

"Willow is not going to like that."

"She can sleep the whole way."

"God, I can hardly wait. I physically miss her."

"I bet."

"How are you? You seem sad."

"I just, I haven't heard back from that reporter and don't know what's going on and I just think it's going to be bad and big and—"

"Why do you care?"

"Why *don't* you care?!"

"Don't snap at me. I do. I did anyway, I'll remind you, before *anyone* else did. But what can we do now? Truth wins out. Isn't that what Grandma Genie used to say?"

"I don't remember her saying that."

"Well, some wise person did. Truth comes out anyway. Chickens and all that."

"Chickens?"

"Yeh, chickens. Come home to roost? Isn't that—"

"Don't you feel bad? I mean, this is going to destroy her career, obviously, but what if she gets really bad? Like becomes bad?"

"Badder?" She's still laughing. "If it was anyone else you wouldn't think that. You'd be at the front of the line screaming about identity theft."

"But it's not anyone else. It's our mother!"

"Your mother."

"Wanting that to be true doesn't make it true." Okay, my tone was a bit more patronizing than I wanted it to be.

"I, holy you're pushing it hey, I don't want it to be true. It just is. She stopped being my mother a long time ago."

I draw back. "I know."

But it was a big nerve to stomp on. "Do you? Do you really truly understand what she did? What it was like growing up over there?"

I had my nerves too: "Of course I fucking do. Don't compete this with me. I was there too."

"No, you weren't." Thuds. Stomping.

"What the hell does that mean?"

"It means you weren't there. You were home, studying. Getting to be at Dad's. All the time. While I was dealing with Renee. By myself."

"That's not fucking fair. You got to be at Dad's when she was gone. And I knew. I got it too. I had to deal with ShitFace and the rest."

"You didn't though," quieter.

I remembered myself. Remembered my little sister. "lyn. I know it was hard. And yeh, you had to deal with her. You were a kid dealing with her, all by yourself. I know that." I take a breath. "And now I am dealing with her. On my own . . ."

"This is not the same thing. Your little guilty conscience whatever you talking to her now is not the same thing as me having to deal with her our whole childhood. Not at all."

I wanted her to understand. "lyn . . ."

But she hung up

lyn

Why do I keep picking up this goddamn phone?

It was a nice morning. I was thinking about work. Vessels techniques craft. Watching old archaeology vids waiting for Yoyo to wake up. Sitting in the backyard listening to the neighbours natter about whether or not to install a hot tub. (My vote was no but no one asked me.)

Another anticlimactic beep. Furiously I paced around. Came in to Yoyo sitting up bleary eyed and barely awake but still managing to look sympathetic. For a moment I was grateful she was there, that I didn't have to have yet another moment all alone. But then I felt it all the way through me, and it sunk down into all the small parts of me, and I wanted her to go, didn't want her to see just how far down I could fall.

I took a shower, got my face in order and drove her home. She rattled on about anatomy this and lab that and something about blood and memory I only heard halfway. We got drive-thru sugary coffees and she got a breakfast sandwich for Matt. A simple gesture so sweet it made me want to cry all over again.

I dropped her at her curb and drove away without looking back. My face fell into tears, the thick blubbery kind, the full throttle kind.

I can feel these feelings and not die.

What if I do though?

It was going to be a hard day. My therapist used to question why I thought these were hard days since I was letting go and emoting so maybe that was easier than when I could not.

But I call bullshit. When a breakfast sandwich makes you can't-stop spit-cry then it's a damn hard day.

I went home to hide under Grandma Genie's blanket that smelt like my baby sister and watched some stupid British cop show I've already watched. I'm still totally committed to the wanky dialogue and wacky twists. No one does cop shows like the British.

I make my moves with Aunty Dell and start a game with Grandma Genie.

I need more sleep. My kid's coming home tomorrow. Or at least, leaving with my stupid sister and her husband to drive here. My stupid sister who's stupid and going to be a block away being stupid. They'll probably be here sometime on Sunday, if not late Saturday. Two to three more sleeps really.

Sad day texts:

Aunty Dell—That one was good. Good job, honey. (Patronizing. June must have told her.)

Grandma Genie—Still coming for supper? [one red heart]

This too makes me cry.

I take a nap right around the time the tough lady cop is getting kicked off the force for being too involved in the case. I doze off or just close my eyes and think of things. Remember. Everything. Nothing. Back and forth, round and round. This is why they call it a spiral. It's like meditation but with all the anxiety, none of the benefits.

June

I literally throw kitchen things into plastic bins, hastily wrap dishes in old newspaper, push linens into garbage bags. At some point moving is just stuffing. I have to run out for more packing tape. This makes me so fucking mad I almost break the cupboard door slamming it closed. Willow and Sigh say nothing as they come in and out loading the trailer.

After a few hours, I thoroughly exhaust myself and make some tea. My tired brain mistakes itself for a calm brain and I check my email. Read over the drafts. Feel like this is good. This is polished. This is ready.

Press Send.

Regret it instantly.

Want to undo it. Want to correct it. Need to look away.

Luckily, I still have cleaning to do.

lyn

Grandma Genie's apartments have always looked the same no matter where she's lived. She's always had the same oversized plants beige furniture same old family photos down the hall pink things in the bathroom. Same tiny table in the kitchen with two chairs that no one ever sits at including her.

She makes me tea and puts too much sugar in it because that's how she thinks I like it. (She's not wrong.)

"How's my dear Willow doing? Home soon, yes?"

"Tomorrow. Well, they're supposed to leave tomorrow."

"Bet you're looking forward to having her home."

I nod.

"And your sister. Boy, I am looking forward to having her back."

I don't scoff outright. Only under my breath.

"And you? What you working on these days?"

I think of how she and I text all the time but say so little.

"Still working on the clay pots. They take a lot of time."

"Are you still talking to that gentleman from the museum? All that stuff is so interesting. We were never taught any of that in school. Nuns only ever said we were simple beasts until we were saved by white men."

"Same. You have to dig to get to the truth."

Grandma nods and makes an agreeing sound. "You'll like this pickerel. Fresh fresh fresh. My cousin's kids are still fishing the lake. Barely getting anything these days but they still try."

"The lake isn't doing too well, hey?"

"No, not doing well at all. Generations my family fished that lake. So many generations. Fished up in what, two, twenty years? And polluted, oh, you wouldn't believe what it looks like, smells like. My cousin says it's an unnatural colour. One of the biggest lakes in the world and full of unnatural colours! Such a shame. Such a crying shame."

I only nod and sip my tea. Grandma Genie would never call herself political but she is as aware as they come. More aware than me, hiding out in my little house feeling sorry for myself.

"Did you hear about that protest march thing? At the Leg? I saw it on the FaceTime. They're marching for the water."

"Facebook, Grandma?"

"Whatever. They got some Elders going to circle the lake again. Or something. I don't know much about that but they're doing a walk up Broadway and then there'll be some speakers."

I arch an eyebrow over my cooling sweet tea. "You wanna go to a march, Grandma?"

"Oh, I don't need to walk all the way up Broadway. But I wouldn't mind hearing the speakers. Go in the crowd there. That would be something."

"Okay. I can take you. When is it?" I don't even know.

"Next week. One afternoon. I'll have to check the time. Oh, I hope it's not too hot."

"We can bring some hats. We can even make a sign or two. I can do that."

"Oh, like one of those signs on those sticks? That they hold up high? Oh yes, that would be something. You'd make them so nice too. You always had such a talent for things like that! You were born to be an artist, you."

"What do you want it to say, Grandma?"

"Oh I don't know, something about not being able to drink money, or eat money, you know, the thing they say about that. I like that. Can you do something like that?"

"You got it."

"Oh, Maarsii, my girl. This makes me happy."

"Me too, Grandma. Me too."

She goes to make more tea and I think of making signs. Been a minute since I made a good protest sign.

I should have told her about the Renee stuff when she came back, but I didn't want to ruin the little smile she had on her face. No, that's not true, I was too chicken. And didn't want to.

Gonna make June do it. Same with Dad. She sure as shit owes me.

June

We didn't leave as early as I wanted to. Took forever to hook up the trailer. Had to park it down the street. Sigh didn't like that. Thing had two deadbolts in one of the richest neighbourhoods in the country but still, that's what he was worried about.

Once we finally got it all set up, we manoeuvred slow to the highway. Took forever for the city to fall away. Then more valleys and highways. I felt restless for the mountains, didn't feel settled until they took up the whole view. It was only then I could breathe a bit.

I always think I'll be bored on drives but three hours in and I'm still just intermittently snoozing and staring out the window. Sigh sings along to a playlist he listens to every time we're on the highway. Willow sleeps under a pile of blankets, wedged between too many garbage bags hastily filled with linens. She hasn't moved since we got in. She set up a little nest and went right to sleep. Zeke pokes his nose out the window on the other side, opened a crack just for him. It's like he's saying goodbye to the mountains too.

I downloaded an audiobook but I haven't even touched it yet. Going over my fight with lyn in my head, what I said, how I said it, what she said. How mad I am. It's been years since we fought like that. I find it so hard to sit with the thought that she is mad at me. I pick up my phone more than once to call her. Then see that she didn't call and get mad all over again.

We're approaching Merritt when Sigh says, "I gotta fill up and empty out."

I roll my eyes. "Sure. How's about you, Zee?" Wet nose on the back of my neck, excitable to the end.

I stretch out and lead Zeke over to the grass. I hold the leash tight, not loving the trucks whizzing by so close.

"How you doing for food? Or do you wanna wait until the next stop?"

"Maybe next. And we got those chips if Princess wakes up and needs something."

"Towing this thing is eating up gas. It's only going to be a few hours at most."

"Don't get too many Rockstars. You're too old."

"Yes, dear."

Willow gets out of the truck, blue hair mashed to the side of her face, phone in hand, she blinks at the sun. I smile at first but that look isn't just tired.

"Aunty. It's out."

4

storm(s)

lyn

Dad's text woke me up and he was at my door before the coffee was even brewed. Had I been more awake I would have realized how strange it all was.

"Where're your tools?" I looked around. Should've known. I assumed he was there to fix the sink again.

He slapped the paper on the table. The thick weekend edition he likes to read cover to cover. Front page colours made her fake tan look even faker. Maybe that was by design. "When did this all happen?"

I don't say anything. June was supposed to tell him, dammit.

"He quoted you."

"Really?"

"June too, and Adele."

"Oh crap."

"I didn't know she was famous!"

I sighed. Picked up then put down the paper without reading. "I told you about her claiming to be Métis or something like that a few years ago, remember? I tried to say something to you know, other people, but didn't hear back from anyone. I tried."

He shook his head. "I thought you were just being . . . I'm sorry. She's always been a little . . . nutty. But this is *nutty* nutty."

"I know it's a lot."

"You know what she said? She said that she was called prairie n-word when she was young. She said that. In some interview they said. I can't believe—I can't believe she would do that."

"I didn't know that, Dad." I scrambled at the pages again. Tried to read the words. Couldn't focus. They all melted together.

"I can't believe she would . . . What did she think? That no one would know? Find out?"

"I don't know, Dad."

"Does June know? That it's out? Didn't she leave today?"

"I don't know." I look down at my phone and check my messages just in case I didn't get a notification. Nothing.

"Have you talked to her?"

"June? Um, no. I talked to Willow yesterday. They were planning on leaving this morning."

"No, your mother."

I shook my head. "No, Dad. It's been years."

He sighed a deep sigh from somewhere far inside him. Ran his hands over his hair. His very grey hair. "I can't believe she would do that."

"Me neither."

"I'm sorry she, I'm sorry you have to deal with this, lynnie."

"Yeh, me too. I'm sorry she did that to you too, that she took your story away. That's . . . I didn't know that. That's horrible."

He only nodded. His hands moved around all confused because there was nothing he could do with them.

June

Sigh came back with an un-asked-for black coffee for me and Willow's favourite gummy worms. Neither of us looked up from our phones. He started the truck and pulled away without a word.

There was the article, long and including many photos of her, links to things she did. There were also a couple op-eds, thought pieces from prominent Indigenous thinkers, ones that always come in when these things happen, one by an Elder—someone from the other side of the country I've always admired, talking about their experience growing up, all the challenges they'd faced and continue to face. There was compare/contrast analysis by an expert in Woodlands style, a timeline—Renee positioned on a long line with other bigger-named pretendian exposés, all with links to those articles. There was even something new about the legacy of Grey Owl, and a reissued editorial by Philip J. Deloria and an excerpt from *Playing Indian*. It was actually a really well thought out collection of think pieces and reactions, thoughtful and accessible. I appreciated it. I would have appreciated it more.

I clicked on socials, felt like I was sneaking in, trying to be quiet. Turned off all my actives. Hiding. I didn't want to look at the mentions but of course I did.

It was as bad as I thought. It was worse. Renee was a hashtag of anger and pain. I try to hold this, for others, all those others so triggered by these things, but I could barely manage my own. Shame.

Did you see what so-and-so said? Here, I'll send it. Willow sent me a link to a filmmaker I knew. Only in passing. But they said: When this happens, we are once again forced to carry the weight of theft and fraud. Let us not turn on each other in this pain. A child is not responsible for a parent's actions. @DrJuneStrangerSavage @lyndenstrangerartist #pretendians @RavenBearclaw #Raven Bearclawisafraud

It was exactly what I needed. Or maybe only wanted. Didn't deserve. I tried to breathe in that little bit of support. Of love. I cried a moment staring out at the now shrinking mountains. The rocky ledges letting me go.

But then made the mistake of clicking on the hashtags. It went something like,

How could they not have known?

What kind of kid lets their parent do that?

They should have said something years ago #silenceisviolence.

Someone should check *their* genealogies.

Apples don't fall far . . .

For a second, I swear I really truly couldn't breathe.

Then,

Willow—Did you see what __ said? That's so cool. You worked with him, right?

Refresh. His picture sprung up. I have known and worked with June Stranger for years. She is a kind, community-minded scholar committed to telling the stories of her people in a good way @DrJuneStrangerSavage.

I looked over at Sigh. His look questioned me. My look panicked.

The next post shot forward: that doesn't mean she's a Neech.

So fast, one after the other. For every one that helped, the other hindered. My anxiety grew.

Shame

"Just breathe," Sigh said, reaching over to my arm. The shock of it, I wanted to pull away, but then the warmth of it felt as good as a hug. I wanted to hide.

Then there were the DMs.

lyn

Sister Adele (no last name given) said, "My grandparents were from Quebec. Came over turn of the century and bought a farm out of St. Adolphe. Never heard anything about anyone being Métis or anything other than French from Quebec. Grandpa was pretty racist actually. Hated wagon burners, as he called them. Said they were lazy. Sorry that's what he said. I'm only telling the truth. I don't agree with him. Just saying what I heard him say."

Daughter Dr. Juniper Stranger-Savage, PhD, said, "I abhor cultural appropriation in all of its forms and unequivocally condemn anyone masquerading a cultural identity they know does not belong to them.

"My father is Métis. My community affiliations within the Michif Nation come from my father's lineage. Growing up, as far as we knew, my mother was white with connections to Quebec and to Mennonite communities. I cannot speak to nor have I seen any genealogy relating to her. Our own paternal genealogy, conducted by the St. Boniface Historical Society and approved by the Manitoba Métis Federation, did not include any family ties on my maternal side, meaning none of her family was Michif from Red River. It's very easy to tell if someone is Michif; historically our births, deaths and marriages were extremely well documented by the Church, something intended to track our demise that has now been reclaimed to help build our eternal legacy.

"But genealogy is only one part. In our Nation, community connections are paramount. I am Michif in my blood but more than that I am Michif in my family and community ties to the people and places around Red River, to my forebearers who fought for our freedom in armed resistances, my lived experience as an Indigenous person and my own ongoing work as a representative of my Nation.

"As a proud Michif person who has been fortunate enough to have always known who I am, I never have and never will stop fighting for Michif rights and sovereignty."

I felt proud of her. Almost forgot I hated her that day.

But it went on and on. Renee had won jobs award shows fellowships all claiming to be Métis descended from a Métis Shaman and super knowledgeable in her culture. At some point she said she had Mi'kmaq ancestry but it looks like she only said that once, but ever after it was on certain bios and she obviously saw them, if not wrote them.

She offered no comment to the article, obviously. But past interviews sounded like she was pillaging my sister for historical information. She dropped words like "matrilineal heritage" and "material culture" like seeds hoping something sprouted. She did a whole series in Woodlands style (which, yes, isn't even

Michif), then another that looked like a bunch of Alex Janvier knockoffs. She also praised June as her daughter, her professor daughter "giving us back our history." She never mentioned me.

They asterisked my s-bombs and corrected my grammar (when I said "fakest" I meant "fakest"! If I'd meant "most fake" I would have said that!), but I can't say they didn't quote me truthfully.

June

There was one from him—Hey. What a shit show? Message me if you need anything. I did tweet in your honour lol.

And one from Renee—Oh isn't that something? Little Miss Warrior. Why can't you ever be that articulate when you're defending me? Oh yeh that's right. You never have!

So many others. Two came in while I was looking. It felt like it was never going to stop.

I saw one, isn't that your mom?? and a new flood came.

I wanted to run. Wanted to push my arms and legs and somehow speed away. Run back to the coast and that mouldy basement apartment and never open the door again.

Instead, I did the smart thing, the thing I hadn't thought that whole time, I put down my phone. Actually, I gave it to Sigh.

"Take it. Take it away from me. Don't give it back."
   "Okay."

"I mean it. No matter what I say. Don't give it back. Chuck it out the window, even."

"How about I just turn it off?"

"Fine, whatever. No, I want to throw it away. Willow, you should get off too. Stop looking. It's a car crash."

"No way! This is the most exciting thing that's ever happened."

"*Exciting*?! This is devastating. There're things in there about me, about your mom. I don't want you reading that."

"Who cares? They don't know us. Let 'em talk."

I couldn't say anything. I could barely breathe again.

"It's not that bad, really. For every one calling you down, there's another saying it's not on you, or quoting your state-ment—I did such a good job on that. Here's one saying it's not on you to even say anything, like the work of the Other type thing and you're her kid, you get a total pass."

"Oh, I wanna see that." I put on my hand out to Sigh.

"Nuh-uh," shaking his head. "I threw it out miles ago. Some semi ran over it."

"Fuck off."

He slowed down, pulled into a rest stop greasy spoon. We were just outside Revelstoke. I had missed so many of the good mountains.

That's not true, there were more, from Renee. Five that I could see, and that was only what I could see. I didn't scroll down. Didn't want to. Couldn't.

Willow: "Oh here come the crazies, Aunty. The white people have officially entered the chat!"

lyn

I message Willow who said she was fine.

I message Yoyo who didn't get back to me.

I call Grandma Genie but there's no answer.

Willow keeps sending me links I don't open.

I delete my socials without looking at them. The apps anyway. Just a quick rip off the band-aid to keep me safe. For now. I make sure it's on silent but keep it close, keep checking.

Unknown numbers call. I let them die in voicemail.

I have a really great text conversation with Kelly of all people. She works in government so is also well versed in folks getting outed for pretending to be something they are not—They think they can get ahead quicker. Like it's a prize and they want something for nothing. But we know. We always know. You can't pretend to be us and fool us. Not all of us anyway.

Aunty Dell finally picked up on the third try. "What? What?! Gosh I'm popular today."

"Are you okay?"

"Me? How about *you*? Thought you'd be fighting mad about all this."

"I don't know what I am. Not in a fighting mood anyway."

"Then best stay off the Facebook—everybody's fighting on there. Well always, but today—whoo-wee!"

"What are they saying?"

"Oh a bunch of people are confused. White people are always clueless when they have to think about this stuff. And people my age have no idea all this lingo and whatnot. So everyone's talking out their arses and no one asked them but they keep talking anyway. One old asshole thought June was talking terrorist crap—do you believe that?"

"I do, actually. Sadly."

"Talk about the idiots running the asylum. Geesh."

"Yeh" is all I can manage.

"Oh don't be sad. Don't be sad, lynnie. This'll all blow over. Folks just like to talk. Makes them feel important, smart, which—whoo-wee, they are not! Let 'em talk. Doesn't do anything to you. They'll be on to something else tomorrow."

"Have you heard from her?"

"My sister? No, I told you."

"No, I mean today. In all this."

"Naw. A cousin told me she got in touch with him a few weeks ago. When all this was starting, I guess. Really random too, like they hadn't seen or talked to each other since they were kids but she told him all about this. He's a lawyer so I guess that's what she was thinking. Not his area though so he couldn't help her. No one else has heard a peep."

"God, I don't want to be thinking of her! She caused all this. She hurt people!"

"Yah, she did. But she's still your mom."

"Yeh." Barely more than a breath.

"Wanna play a game?"

"You're an addict."

"Do you blame me? The shit I have to put up with. Come on! Kicking yer arse would make me feel better."

It was the nearest I came to laughing that whole day.

After a few moves, Yoyo texts to check on me. She does a brief compassionate back-and-forth, then blurts in with—I think Matt is going to break up with me. What am I going to do???!!!

I leave her on Read while I make myself a huge bowl of cereal and only eventually text back that she's full of shit.

The unknown callers keep calling but I am not that stupid. Or sadistic.

June doesn't call.

June

I don't get it. What's the big deal?—Karen from Orangeville.

We inch closer to Banff and I use Sigh's phone to call Dad. "Oh I'm fine. Fine," he says. "Have you talked to your sister?"

This is reverse racism, pure and simple. I thought it wasn't supposed to matter what race you are?!?!?!—Mike from Ottawa.

Then, Grandma Genie—Oh what nonsense. Your mother, I loved that girl, but really, sheesh. Did your sister tell you about the protest?

This is because she fooled them for so long. They're only mad because they have egg on their face now!—Joe from Manitoulin Island.

Aunty Dell—What does this matrilineal mean?

She has the right to make whatever art she wants. I thought we lived in a free country!—Carrie from Calgary.

Then I'm tired.

I tell myself this is why I don't call lyn.

It's almost as if race doesn't matter. Hmm??? Weird!!!—Kevin from Windsor.

I take over driving. Sigh needs to close his eyes and I need a distraction. Willow is still texting with everyone—Yoyo, and her mom of course. Everyone seems to be coping. I'm trying to watch what's left of the mountains and their perfect sky.

My eyes start glazing over as the light fades and I find a nice enough motel near Medicine Hat. Willow and I check in while Sigh grabs his vape and goes to walk Zeke, passes me back my phone with a look.

By the time he's back, Willow is under her bedcover watching some movie on her tablet. And I'm all caught up on every single post made since I last checked.

I should call her now. My sister. Should

Instead I watch some movie on the room's old TV. Rest my eyes during the commercials. Sigh's snoring. So is Zeke.

Yoyo texts me—She's fine but you should ask her yourself. And hey can I ask you something about men?

I turn it off. Vow to give it back to Sigh in the morning. Maybe check one more time and then give it back.

I close my eyes at the third repeat for some flooring ad and don't seem to open them again.

lyn

Renee didn't last long in the Caribbean (the accent lasted a few years though). She got "stuck" in Toronto (ten-month layover). Then came over one Sunday. Dad and Kelly didn't even know she was coming. Little Yoyo toddled around and cried at the stranger in her house. Renee looked tired, said she'd got a loft in the Exchange and I should pack my stuff.

"Don't go." June followed me to my room. "It's too far for school."

"I can take the bus. It won't take that long."

"But what about your art club? That would go too late."

"I'll figure it out. Besides, who needs art club if I'm living in a real live artist loft!"

The place was dingy and falling apart. The kitchen was a long folding table, hot plate and stand-alone sink. Her roommate (the guy that was living there and let us stay) did weird art with old mannequins (that I would always mistake for ghosts in the dark).

Renee said she was tired of the singer-songwriter thing and wanted to try visual art. She spent all her money on brand-new paints, brushes, an easel that cost more than a month's rent. I'd have dinner at Dad's before I took the bus home from school because there was never any food there. June rolled her eyes at me whenever I left but I didn't care. Not really. Renee and I spent the weekends rooting fabric stores for offcuts we would stretch over poorly nailed-together boards for her canvases, and sometimes, if I was very careful, she would even let me paint too.

My semester wasn't even over yet when Renee got into a fight with the weird artist and had to move out. She found a place not far from Dad's.

I was excited at first (more fool me, hey), I thought she was getting her shit together. She talked about getting a job at a gallery, all these people she knew who were going to help her out. I was close enough I didn't have to take the bus to school. We set the place up with cool thrift store finds, but the mattress on the floor was barely made up before CokeHead moved in.

Renee was in love again and I was back on the couch—a new old one, a sad thing she drenched with perfume 'cause it reeked of old cigarettes.

She had gone to high school with CokeHead. Knew him before she even knew Dad. She never felt understood by anyone until CokeHead. Never knew men could be so sensitive until Coke-Head. She told me this while he was in the next room (because he never left) like she was selling me something—he was so nice, cool, kind and talented (glorified eighties cover band). Renee fell really hard (understatement).

He had a badly covered up swastika tattoo on the back of his left hand, vague stories about unnamed children out in the world, a side hustle selling hard drugs and the aforementioned raging coke habit, but yeh, the guy was personable, I'll give him that.

He basically lived with us after like a day. He was going to make his millions playing bad music with cheap guitars. Renee said I could go to his shows as soon as they played an all ages, but I wasn't in a hurry. He spent every spare minute strumming on his not-hooked-up electric guitar and stopping and starting cassettes on Renee's old stereo. Practising, she told me, with an oblivious smile.

He was also high all the time. He'd shoot up right in front of us, pull out all his gear at the kitchen table like it was a normal thing to do. One time he tugged me over and told me to keep my finger on his neck vein while he did it, to feel his heart pulse faster and faster as he injected, dropped his head back and exhaled.

"Isn't that neat?!" he shouted with a laugh. Eyes brightest.

I wasn't an idiot. I knew it wasn't neat. I knew I couldn't tell June 'cause she'd tell Dad and be mad at Renee. My sister never came over. She stayed far away, even though we were only a few blocks apart. I don't remember her and CokeHead ever even being in the same room. She knew of him, of course, just not everything.

But really, and I know this sounds awful, but it wasn't always that bad. I mean sure there were syringes everywhere but Renee was also really happy. She was working all the time, doing amazing things with abstracts, and yes this was also when she joined the Afro drum group. She was electrified, electrifying. Would take me to galleries and shows downtown and in the Village. It felt like an education, and really was. She knew absolutely everything about the Inuit art collection in the city gallery (insert sarcastic comment) and started working with MFA students in the university. I was proud delighted loved every minute. Almost every.

"The world is so alive, lynnie! Art is truth and beauty and life. And it's everywhere. Waiting for us to take it."

She wasn't wrong.

June

The hills rolled away and flattened into the prairie crops. I know the yellow stuff is canola. Used to call it mustard as a kid but one time Renee corrected us. I remember being surprised she would know what farmers' fields are full of. Or is it the blue stuff that's canola?

I did give Sigh my phone back. Am only imagining what they are saying now.

I don't know what any other crop is. Sunflowers, obviously. Wheat. There is neither here though.

We pass Swift Current and the signs start advertising Moose Jaw. I am tempted to stop. Would love to soak in the hot springs awhile. But I know there's no escaping. We're going home.

I am going home.

I will be home soon.

lyn

Über-talented CokeHead really lived his über-talented life to the fullest, and shockingly the good times don't last when you have a shoot-up coke habit. But still I didn't leave.

I knew I should have. Knew I should have walked the few blocks to Dad's place where I had space siblings supper and was always welcome. But I didn't leave.

I didn't leave when CokeHead and Renee came home too late, made too much noise and kept me up while they talked, made food, fought. I didn't leave when I fell asleep in class or didn't go altogether because the apartment was always quiet in the mornings.

I didn't leave when Renee screamed in the night and had a black eye in the morning. Or when he told me I had those nice full lips that were in style now and would make a killing if I ever wanted to be an "escort or something." I didn't even respond, only looked over at Renee. Who had heard. But pretended not to. I still didn't leave.

No, I finally left after one Sunday at my dad's. I was over there a lot, really. To stay in a bed that was all my own all the time and rent movies with June. To play with my little baby siblings who I thought were truly neat. To be a kid. But never for too long.

I was walking up the basement stairs when I heard Dad and Kel having a quiet conversation that sounded like a fight. I stopped before the squeaky step and listened.

"She shouldn't go back there. Something's going to happen, Jer."

"Renee would never let anything happen."

"She's already let so much happen. She's not . . . She's a horrible mother. You have to make lyn stay."

"I can't do that. She wants to be with her mom."

"Her fucking mom's only keeping her 'cause she can't pay child support."

"That was the deal. We each get one. She doesn't have any money, Kel."

"That's not our problem, Jer. And not even the issue anymore. lyn has to get out of that place."

"We'd never get a dime from her."

"I don't even care anymore."

I don't know why this was the blow that did it. Or why it stays with me, even now. Sometimes the biggest thing only sounds small when you say it out loud. Inside of me, it was huge, took over, became everything.

I always thought Renee couldn't bear to be without me. That June could go be with Dad as long as I was with her. I thought it was 'cause she loved me. Thought it was 'cause she loved me more. The most

But it was about money.

I packed my bags while she was who knows where. She didn't call for three days. When she did, my dad told her I was out even though I was sitting next to him.

I wasn't there when things got really bad. When too-high-to-know-a-thing CokeHead tried to kill her (twice) and someone called the cops (once). I wasn't there

We saw her about a week later. She had gone to stay with Aunty Dell, who called us to come. Her face was bruised and bandaged. Her wrist was in a cast.

"He has a disease," she told us. And cried and cried.

Aunty Dell told us not to worry. "Her meds will even out soon."

I thought she meant painkillers.

June

We're filling up outside Brandon when I ask for my phone back again.

"If you're sure."

"I'm sure."

"If you are sure you're sure."

"Give me my fucking phone."

"You said . . ." He tries to be playful.

But I am humourless. "Forget what I said. Stop it. I am a whole grown-assed adult."

He hands it over and takes up Zeke's leash and his vape. "You don't have to do this to yourself, you know."

"I know." Too harsh.

Willow in the back seat: "Oh Aunty, there's this old guy from Quebec jus' going off. So confused. It's hilarious. Here, I'll send it to you."

"The fact that you're enjoying this so much troubles me."

"Oh please, the warriors got this. Things are changing. The whole world is changing. This is exciting!"

She's so young. I don't think I was ever that young.

I wait for it to open. The slow warm-up of the screen.

I am calm, I am peace, I am ready.

It's more of the same. Tired already. Me and the dialogue. People coming to her defence, not the sort of people anyone would want on their side. Everyone fighting. Angry and not listening. Nothing new.

It'll take a few days for the thoughtful think pieces to emerge. Mindful response takes time. And also, there is so much more going on in the world. Already the feed looks full of other things. So many more other violences to recover from.

I click on an article on a pipeline protest in northern BC, another on a dam in the north, then fall down a rabbit hole of global water sovereignty and its overlaps with the safety, and lack thereof, of Indigenous people, particularly women and Two-Spirit people.

We pass Portage la Prairie as I am reading about a river in Australia that has the same history with missing persons as mine does in Winnipeg.

Mine. Have always called it my river. My home.

Yeh, guess it is time.

Home.

Happening anyway.

lyn

Hard clay shards of old pottery have been found along waterways throughout the province this city our territory. I have a friend who takes her kids out often to go find some. They have a large collection. They share it with my other friend at the museum. I've gone with them a few times. Have dug out long ceramic blades, curved ridges of what were once bowls, now broken pieces with no hope of ever getting put back together. Easily mistaken for nothing at all. I have used them to model what I do. To study and try to re-create the same pigments and designs. Some are easier to figure out than others.

The oldest known pottery found in what is now called North America is around four thousand years old. It was excavated along the Savannah River in Georgia. Much about the ancient civilizations of what has always been called Turtle Island is unknown (or *unproven*), but we do know that they were further along in math astronomy farming than many other places in the world at the same time. Far from being primitive hunter-gatherers, they had cities townships cultures so many cultures. Digging through this history is a treasure hunt. Vessels found more precious than gold.

The pottery of the Savannah River, like all pottery, goes hand in hand with the water. Water being the source of all life everywhere, and of course sacred to all First Nations (and, well, everyone on the planet, right?). In our stories, water is regarded as a woman, as it's often said women are water carriers. Earth is also a woman.

Fun fact: There are strong indications that children played with clay and that their creations would be fired alongside more useful materials. Something I find so indulgent and endearing.

Another fun fact: Clay was used to line the enormous bell jars that have been found along the Red River. These were dug deep in the earth, had a large base and a narrow opening, and what would have been a wooden ladder poking out the top. The walls were covered by the same river clay only not fired, obviously. Still, it hardened and stayed.

These bell jars were used to store food, surplus from crops housed deep in the earth where it could stay cool and fresh. Traditionally, agriculture was seen as women's work, or at least planned and overseen by women. Tended to and harvested by all, then after everyone had their fill, stored in the bell jars. What was inside was considered community property, there for anyone to take, so if you didn't have enough, you'd take your bowl over to the bell jar and fill up.

These are the lessons I am pulling from the earth. These are the gestures that in every way have kept us alive.

And yes, I am fully aware I am disassociating. Can you blame me?

June

If you go down Highway 1 west from Winnipeg, you start with the bushy greens of Manitoba. The evergreens fade quick though as the land calms and seems to still into Saskatchewan, where everything is as flat as a board, goes on and on, and is somehow forever yellow. Next, Alberta breaks the earth open, the grasses deepen back to green shades and the ground starts to roll and roll, until just past Calgary when the Rockies finally emerge in the distance. The mountains are sudden and everywhere. They cradle and cuddle the road like they're never going to let you go. They block the sun, fill up the windows and become everything.

Going east is all that in reverse. Anticlimactic. Downhill. Backwards.

I was sad to leave the mountains. Always cry when they finally release me, then gaze into the minty hills with their tidy patterns. Down that long straight line of the prairie highway to, eventually, finally, home. Red River Territory. This land is a crater of rich watershed not much above sea level. Before the last ice age, this place was all an ocean but that dried and left fertile earth, this bush, these lakes and rivers. It all still thinks like an ocean, moves like water, draws things in and never lets go. Colder than Mars in the winter, hotter than hell in summer. Winnipeg. Home. No one has ever asked me why I left. We all know why we leave.

Since I was a kid, I've only been here while in motion, passing through, stopping over, visiting.

The thing about leaving is at some point it stops. The leaving becomes left and then you're only someplace else.

lyn

After CokeHead endangered us both (all) and went to prison for trying to kill her, Renee wanted to go visit him. She asked me if I wanted to come along.

We were at a greasy spoon by Aunty Dell's, the three of us, when she said this and June sprang up and said, "You're fucking nuts!"

Renee didn't miss a beat. "Don't you talk to me like that, young lady. I am still your mother. Sit down and stop making a show of yourself."

My sister turned to me. "I'll be outside."

I finished my BLT and paid for everything with the only twenty I had. Renee didn't have anything.

She couldn't walk the two blocks so called Aunty Dell to come pick her up. My sister didn't say a word as we waited. Aunty pulled up and I helped Renee into the car.

Aunty Dell knew as soon as she saw our faces. Or maybe it was only Renee's face. "What happened?"

"Oh Dell, she hates me. My own daughter hates me. After everything I've been through."

Aunty Dell gave me a look of sympathy and waved me away.

I closed the door as Renee was saying, "I only ever tried to do right by them. I tried so hard."

Aunty Dell called us later that night. Talked to me 'cause June said she was reading and couldn't come to the phone.

"Renee's okay. I didn't want you to worry."

I didn't tell her that I wasn't worried. Not anymore.

Renee got her own place in Aunty Dell's building and got a job at the grocery store down the street. She always had groceries then which was kind of weird. Which is weird that it was kind of weird but only in hindsight. She had a good few years. Okay, one good year, for sure. Her bruises faded, her arm healed, and she took me to galleries and shows again. I went over to her house to paint or play with collage.

I would take the bus up there by myself 'cause June couldn't be bothered.

Dad's place was run amuck with young kids. My sister was busy with school and obsessing about university. Renee was my best friend. I had her all to myself for a change. For a while anyway.

Late afternoon texts:

Willow—jus passed the perimeter. Eeeeeeee. Why does it look like fall here?

Yoyo—I can't believe she's going to be here???!?!?!?!?!?!?!?! [also a couple memes that were not even funny. Or had any cats.]

Dad—need ride ther?

Me—it's around the corner!

Dad—well I don't know what you wan

Me—?

Dad—??

Me—I'll meet you ther

June

Dad is waiting in his truck when we pull up. It's only been about a year since I've seen him in person but he looks aged. He gets out with a grunt and comes over, limping on his knee a bit more. Kelly had already called me to say she had a meeting but would come by in the morning.

I want to run in the house but Zeke needs to smell everything in the small front yard and Dad's seen it already so he's asking us about the drive. Working up to ask us how we are, to talk about it, I bet. I wonder where my sister is and why she didn't meet us, too.

The trim needs new paint, what was once grey now nearly white. There's some brown siding I don't love and the porch is smaller than it looked on the video. There's a couple of those boring evergreen bushes and a whole lot of weeds. I've been known to kill a cactus so this is going to be rough. Kelly gardens. I'll have to ask her.

Willow paces the grass in circles as her mom comes into view. My sister jogs the last few steps and takes her kid in her arms. That's when Willow starts crying. When the still-a-child sobs into her mom's shoulder with all the worries she's been holding in. I didn't even know the kid was upset but yeh, she must have been. Of course. Under that tough exterior. Like her mom.

I am insanely jealous of this mothering. I want to go up too. I want to say sorry sorry sorry but I turn and walk into my new old house instead. Give my dad an excited look, like I am excited.

The front door is old, maybe even original. The cut glass beautiful. I feel a sense of hope. But inside, the carpet is as brown as the siding, the plaster falling off the wall above the front window, no less than three wet spots on the ceiling. I give Sigh a long look but he points at the back, "Look at this glass." It's true, all the windows have the same floral pattern in stained glass, dark blue and red centre, could look like an infinity symbol if you squint your eyes right. The back one catches the evening light. Okay, this might work.

Dad keeps talking about all the easy fixes and cleanups but I go down the door to the basement, the creepy and smells mouldy basement. The foundation obviously cracked. Zeke finds something in a very dark corner that I don't let him eat. Then I rush him up the steep old stairs and close the door behind us.

Sigh smiles at me. I say nothing.

The stairs to the second floor are creaky and two are too wobbly for my liking. The carpet goes all the way to the attic, relentless and without padding underneath either. Probably glued. Even I know that's going to be a bitch to get off.

The main bedroom is narrow, the other two, small. It's small to me and I'm coming from Van where everything is the size of a closet.

One doesn't even have a closet and is painted a dark blue I would have loved as a teenager.

The attic stairs are worse than the others. But up there it's all wood panelled, faded, but with two big windows on either side of a long peaked ceiling. Built-in closets line one side, and a desk and shelves on the other. It smells like a dry sauna with all the sun pouring in. Sigh comes up behind me.

"What do you think?"

This time I smile for real.

lyn

Willow quiets and we sit on the steps. I can hear Dad going through the house, imagine June's look in her silence. She is no doubt fixated on all the problems and potential problems. I can see the brown siding in her grimace. The railing loose on the stairs.

But I am counting the clouds and holding my kid. The good feelings are easy to have and know you will not die. I never think these feelings will kill me. Opposite actually. I think they will go away too fast. And they do.

My kid. I could see it as she came up to me. Saw my sister's stress too, but I really wanted my kid first. Knew she needed me. Willow's too-young face crumpled down. Tired. Sad. I ran up and held her quick. Pulled her close and smelled the top of her head that is my most favourite smell in the whole world. She sobbed but only quiet. So only I could hear.

One time when she was little, littler, like twelve, she got into a car accident with her dad. It was only minor. He said on the phone she was fine. And she was. But when I got there, to the side of the street beside his wreck of a car, that's when she cried. Her skinny shoulders shook and she couldn't even find words. Didn't have to.

"Wanna see my photos?" Willow says finally.

"Boy do I!" Knowing she's already posted or sent or shared most of them with me.

But one more time, I look at the sky the inlet my kid perfect and posed. So well lit. As good as the first time I saw them.

I think she somehow grew in the last six weeks. Looks older. When she was small, whenever a teacher or her even her dad took her picture, she always seemed to look older in them. In the pictures I took she always looked like a baby. My baby.

And she is. But she's also not.

We go into the house and look around. It smells like old carpet and mould. I can hear June upstairs creaking along the floor-boards. Not talking. Looking so forcefully. I find Dad in the dining room staring at the ceiling. A dull discoloured patch. Could be wet, what do I know? (Not that much really.) I look out the back window at the tall weeds, two narrow gravel strips that used to be a whole driveway.

My sister comes down looking more relaxed. She must have seen something she likes or something she can work with. Her house. The place she will live and maybe make a home. So close to me. I haven't dared think about it all the way until now.

Who knows how long it will last but

how great it'll be to have her around.

June

Dad points up at a wet spot. "Could be a leak. Could be nothing. Keep an eye on it."

My brief joy deflates. So much house.

"We used to live in one of these, you know. You were small."

I am intrigued. "Where was that? I can almost remember."

"lynnie was born there. So you were what, two? It was on Bannerman."

"Bannerman! Like in the North End? Renee lived in the North End?!"

"She didn't last a year. Then we moved to St. Norbert."

"I remember that one." I'm still baffled. "Can't believe Renee let you move her to the North End."

"It was the eighties. Men were men back then. What I said is what happened."

"And Grandma Genie told her to?"

"Yeh, she helped."

"How is Grandma? I didn't get ahold of her yesterday."

lyn comes up behind me: "She wants to do protests now."

"What?!"

"Yup. Total activist. Probably getting in a Facebook fight as we speak." I talk to my sister all the time, but I always know how much I have missed her when I see her in person.

"When did this happen?"

lyn sighs, still not looking right at me though. "She found out about a demonstration at the Leg. You have to take her with me."

I feel the tears in my eyes. There is so much. "Okay. Weird but okay."

"Yup, she's all up on everything. Doing all the things." My sister shrugs. She looks thinner than she was a year ago. Older. The so many things FaceTime doesn't pick up.

"Son of a bitch. She's making us look bad." I try to be like lyn, to be light.

She laughs a bit. Politely.

Dad and Sigh take Willow to start unloading the trailer.

My sister turns to me, finally. Asks me gently, "You okay?"

I nod. Swallow the lump in my throat. "I'm sorry I didn't mean . . ."

Didn't even know what I was going to say but she goes, "Me neither. Me too . . ." Skips over all of it and we know.

We don't have to say a thing. We know it all.

lyn

Yoyo brings her boyfriend and the men get to the last of the heavy stuff. Matt and Sigh as Dad oversees. I don't think I've ever heard Matt talk, he's so quiet. Takes direction well though. Makes sense if he's with Yoyo. She was born bossy.

My sisters and I open beers and sit on the front porch's unscreened sides. Willow scrolls her phone and I watch Sigh explain to Dad what all the big custom-made collectable crates are.

I nudge June so we can all watch Dad try to not laugh as he says, "So you have . . . toys?"

Sigh blusters up something like "limited edition" and "investment" and just when I think he's gonna get it (a Dad "get it" which is really only a disapproving look that somehow makes you feel really bad), he opens up a crate and Dad is enthralled. "Oh I remember this cartoon. lynnie—this was your favourite, right?"

He turns to me but I recoil, knowing how my sister feels about said toys, very intelligently say, "Don't drag me into this." (This makes me giggle even if no one else does.)

June

I put the sheets on the mattress and set it on the floor. We brought the bed frame and will set it up tomorrow. Need all new living room furniture though, and Sigh wants to rip out the kitchen completely.

"It's not just the counters. These cupboards are falling apart. Might as well rip them out while we taking out the old appliances. And remove this wall to the dining room. It's not like we ever use a dining room."

"Never had a dining room."

"See. We won't miss it."

"Sounds like a lot of work. And mess."

"It's a day's demo at the most. Your dad and Matt said they'd help. You women folk can sit around and make us sandwiches." He gets undressed and I pull the comforter out of a garbage bag.

"Sit around and bitch about you, you mean."

"I would love nothing more."

My eyes linger on his beautiful back for a beat, before: "This carpet is old and gross."

"We can rip it out if you want. Or I can rent one of those cleaners. It'll be good as new with a good clean." He takes a corner of the blanket to help me.

"I think the foundation is cracked."

"Naw, that's stone. It'll be fine." He even smooths it down and fluffs the pillows.

"Famous last words."

"I had a good look. It's fine."

I am not convinced. But he plops down on the mattress and pulls me onto his lap. "I was going to go all man cave in the basement but it's too damp. The toys will have to go up here." His big warm arms around me.

I stiffen. "Where?"

"I'll put them in the smaller bedroom. With the closet."

"We're giving the toys their own room?"

"It'll be my office." He cuddles closer. Trying to get away with it all. Succeeding.

"Your office to do what?"

"I don't know. Office stuff."

"Video games."

"Likely."

I consider working with this. "We can put something else in there too. Like a hideabed. Make it a guest room too."

"I get one room!" But he's only joking. His lips find my neck.

"You can play games from the comfort of a hideabed," I say with a giggle.

"The other room can have a hideabed." He leans over.

"I thought that was going to be Zeke's room." I lean back.

When Sigh and Zeke are snoring loudly, I make the mistake of looking.

There's a new thread from some white supremacist douchey douche saying what's the big deal? and how appropriation is so A-OK because everybody does it and artistic freedom freedom freedumbs.

Basically, his argument hinges on whitewashing being totally acceptable because it's all made for consumption and the biggest consumers are people like him. Oh, and disagreements like this aren't necessary because it's confusing and hurts his feelings, and you know, I can't believe the phrase has taken so long to enter into this dialogue but of course it always wields its ugly head, they should just *GET OVER IT*.

I take a deep breath and then another.

I turn to shopping for area rugs to calm down.

Kelly texts that she'll bring breakfast over, see the house.

For a minute, I had forgotten where I was.

lyn

Willow and I stay up late and catch up on our show. The one we couldn't watch without each other and were waiting for. During the montages (why are there always so many montages?), she updates me on all her new friends from program who she's been talking about all summer. Then ahead to school and the year coming.

I fall asleep before the end credits of the last episode (obviously super invested) and she nudges me sometime after. I limp up the stairs with her because I need to tuck her in. Need to get the blankets snug and tight around her, each side and of course her feet. Willow has always needed her feet covered.

"Thanks, Mom," she whispers in the dark. "Love you."

"Love you more." I click on her night light. The one with the moon glowing green then blue. The one not turned on all summer.

June

My new house creaks in unfamiliar ways. I can't ever sleep my first night in a new place, home or hotel, first night is a restless fight with pillows. My snoring bedmates do not have this problem.

I nudge my husband over on his side. Hope the snoring isn't getting worse or a sign of something. He does vape too much.

I will myself not to look up snoring in midlife.

Something moves on the third floor. I swear to god something moved. I look over but Zeke is still stretched out at my feet, taking up too much room. Groaning when I kick him but not moving.

If it was a ghost he would have woken up. I think.

I will myself not to look up ghosts and dogs.

Turn over again. Turn it all over.

Years ago, back when only brown people were talking about cultural appropriation, I took a creative writing class with a very white professor who wrote fiction almost exclusively about characters of colour. Most of them were Indigenous, actually, which is what I thought she was when I signed up. To her credit, she wasn't pretendianing but a quite proud British ex-pat. One of those who left when she was three and still had the accent type people. In the class there were no less than three middle-aged white ladies writing coming-of-age novels from the point of view of young East Asian characters. This was maybe 2012, no word of a lie. Feels like a hundred years ago.

It bothered me and I thought of saying something but didn't have the words yet. Until this one fine day, the exercise was for us to write from the point of view of someone not of our own race or culture. I wrote from a white perspective, which I also am, so was cheating, really. When we reviewed and shared, I brought up my discomfort, however sheepishly, about the whole cultural appropriation thing, which at that time was still being framed as a "controversy." The prof seemed to thicken her posh accent as she shook her head and didn't even let me finish my point before interjecting: "Oh no, I don't think that's relevant at all. We're artists and this is just *what we do*."

Patronizing, dismissive, but also concise. I usually appreciate concise, especially from writers, most of whom do tend to go on, but really, we know this is complete bullshit, right? That's not confusing, is it? That doesn't hurt anyone's feelings too much? I mean yeh, of course we can do whatever we want, all of us can, all the time, but that's not what she was talking about—she was talking about consequences. She wanted to do whatever she wanted without having to hear about the consequences. None of us are free of that, ever, nor should we be.

For Renee, I think this is about how she never thought she had enough, was enough, good enough on her own, maybe. She always wanted more, more love, recognition, attention. She was always moving, couldn't stop, always had to do something new, maybe because no matter what she tried, she didn't, couldn't, fill herself up.

I can relate to that.

Or am I projecting myself on her? My problem is I am always trying to understand, can never understand enough.

The light changes out my window. New window. Morning coming. The early light of summer. A clear view to the whole sky.

No elm trees on this street. Just noticed.

5

back home

lyn

My kid wanders downstairs as I finish my coffee, late for her (to be fair it's noon). "Morning, Sleeping Beauty!"

"I didn't sleep in all summer. I was in program. Plus, time change!" So defensive.

"I know, I know." (Retreat! Retreat!) "You hungry? I bought bacon."

"Ugh, bacon's disgusting. And killing our planet never mind the sweet innocent pigs. They're as intelligent as three-year-olds, you know!"

"Eggs then?"

She huffs then slams the bathroom door behind her.

I missed her so much.

I fry her up some tofu I forgot I had (smells fine). She sits at the table and picks at it. We talk about groceries and school supplies, then catch up on neighbourhood gossip:

"I think the Young Neighbours broke up. I haven't seen her in weeks, and he's always bringing a case of beer in when he comes home. Lady with the good white dog got those planters. Everyone's into these planters these days."

"Above-ground gardening has been around forever, Mom. It makes plants grow better. Better drainage."

"Who taught you that?"

"Grandma Kelly has them."

"Really? Where? I've never noticed."

"They're like right in front of their house."

I shrug. "Whatever. I don't get it. I like grass."

"Yah ya do." She giggles at her own joke (where'd she learn that?), then shows me her phone. "Look at this shirt. I want it so bad. Isn't it beautiful?"

"It is. Very Willow. Never has a shirt been more Willowable than that shirt."

"Will you buy it for me?"

"No way. I don't have name brand kind of money."

"Not even for back to school?"

"Not even maybe. Ask your dad."

"He's cheaper than you."

"Um, we prefer to use the word *frugal* now.

Old Neighbours are building a new deck out back. I think I heard them say they're getting a hot tub."

"Ew, old people soup."

"Least of my worries with those two."

The neighbourhood gossip is a tradition Shannon started with Willow and me (not that I haven't always been nosy). They gave everyone cute pragmatic nicknames—good white dog (friendly), bad white dog (barks), Young Neighbours (south side), Old Neighbours (north), cross the street new people (been there five years now), old guy on the corner (best yard and garden, hands down), and we'd all know who the other was talking about by this simple information. Shannon always joked that gossiping was their culture. June has told me how historically gossiping has been a form of cultural exchange to refine norms and mores. I just think I work at home and am alone a lot and it's fun.

"Cross the street new people painted their house!"
Willow doesn't look up from her phone.
"Yeh . . ." My eagerness and voice fade out.
She glances out the window: "Stupid colour."
Sooo my kid.

June

My sister calls as we're sitting out on our porch. Enjoying our first proper porch-sitting and watching the neighbourhood. Smelling the smells of freshly cut grass, prairie city and that cold edge of fall creeping in.

lyn: "How's it going?"

"All right."

"No ghosts then?"

"Don't even say that!"

"All unpacked?"

"Apparently we're doing the whole kitchen first." I roll my eyes at my husband, who shoots me his million-dollar grin.

"Oh, you must love that."

"Meh. How are you? Happy to have your girl home?"

"Yeh, but."

Somewhere in her hesitation it all comes back. The wave of it, between us. "Did you see that article out last night?"

"Naw, I'm avoiding all that shit."

"Lucky bastard." And I mean it.

"What'd it say?"

"You don't wanna know."

"Right on that."

Sigh takes my empty glass and goes inside to pour another. I love that man. "I'm worried about this, lyn."

"I'm not thinking about it."

"Why doesn't that surprise me."

lyn

I have 48 vessels. 48 in my collection of pots with personality.

I should think of a better name for them, something studious for the grant application.

48 vessels of varying sizes, densities, widths, lengths.

48 vessels in the various styles of ancient North American pottery.

Yes. Granting bodies love a good history lesson.

Material examples of culture.

48 examples of material culture showcasing the varying, evolving and differentiating styles of the ancient pottery of North America.

That's it. I don't know if *differentiating* is the right word but it sounds good (long = good).

I have been working in multiples of 4 and by extension 8.

4 is a sacred number, represents a whole bunch of things—seasons, directions, phases of life, moon, colours. Some say these colours also represent the races of the world but I call big bullshit on that. It's reductive and illogical (and pretty racist). Ancient Teachings were anything but that—they were incredibly expansive and inclusive. Also (arguably) they didn't know about persons outside this continent or if they did, they wouldn't've seen them in the same way Europeans seem to see everyone else (reductively).

8 is two groups of 4 (obvs) but as well, we are currently in the 8th generation from contact. There is a prophecy called the 8th fire that refers to this as the time of transition and empowerment.

8 × 4 is 32, which is a full moon cycle—full moons happen every 28 days but last for 4 days so 32

8 × 8 is 64 and makes up a 4-spoke circle if each spoke and curved side has 8 in it. Maybe that's what I am going for. I will see how it feels when I have 64 vessels.

I have a thing with numbers. I know I need structure, but also know I will immediately rebel against any structure imposed (even if it's imposed by me) so I try to sneak around this with numbers. Because then it feels like play. And I have to approach projects with play. I play at first until I figure out what I am doing. I still don't know what I am doing.

I start with vessel 49. I feel like coiling today, will roll the wetted earth in my hands and build and build until it looks like something. Small, dense, as thin as it will let me go. Will work to 56 then

I will fire this last group—I am firing in groups of 8. Multiples of, as many as I can fit in my old kiln, which isn't many. Though maybe I will build a fire outside instead. The real old way.

I put them side by side in variations to see how they fit together best. Fit next to one another. "Best" here being arbitrary as all art is arbitrary. It only has to be best to me. It only has to feel right to me. Then I only have to explain it like I meant to do that all along (and boom = art!).

The explaining part doesn't come naturally to me and has jinxed my process more than once when I've tried to make sense of it too soon. I put off articulating the art so as not to disrupt (jinx) the process, and because I hate it that much. It's really only a small part. Necessary only for grants or artistic statements. Explaining feels like defending. I hate defending.

I think the whole point of art is to see. Maybe you see what the artist wants you to see, maybe you see something else. Doesn't matter. We really only ever see ourselves anyway. Anything we read or hear—books sculpture painting music—is only what we are, us reflected back to us. Who cares what the artist intended as long as you got something out of it.

Defending is for the defensive. It's for those who want to make what we do important and on purpose and meaningful, not for those of us who think it's all those things already.

The secret is we're all only playing, happy accidents (happy until we have to write a grant proposal). Explaining takes the mystery out of the whole thing. The greats never explained themselves. Picasso da Vinci Monet never wrote artistic statements. Or if they did, they've been lost to history. Why? Because they don't matter. Only the art matters.

Vessel 49 is small, oblong and rough. It will need to dry for a few days and then will need a lot of sanding. Vessel 49 is trying not to take up too much space, wants to hide and not exist, is sorry for existing. It has a troublesome seam at the bottom, something I have tried to fix over and over. Will likely crack or break altogether in the heat, might be completely, unfortunately useless.

That's the worst part. When I can't even soak and remake them. As long as I can keep doing something with it, then it feels okay.

June

"Hi, Grandma, how you doing?"

"Oh good. Good. You're here, then? All safe?"

"Yeh, all safe, all good. You should come see the house before it looks like a war zone."

"Why would it look like a war zone?"

"Oh, we're gutting the whole thing, apparently."

"You have time for that? I thought you had some big fancy job?"

"I do. Sigh is working on the kitchen, for now. It's only the kitchen. I'm exaggerating."

"Doesn't he have a job?"

"Not yet. But he'll find something. We just got here."

"Mmm." She says her *mmm*s like Dad, or more like he does like her. My Mamere Annie used to do that too. Our whole family, really, can make a sound seem like a lecture.

"It's good, Grandma, it's good. We're okay for money." Then, pivot: "Want me to come get you later? Bring you by?"

"Oh, can't today, I have yoga later and then I have to finish my knitting. Why don't you come get me tomorrow morning. You can drive me to the Friendship Centre. I've been making mittens and scarves for their program."

I'm surprised, but only a little. "Okay, sure. What time?"

"Come by nine. Bring me a double-double."

I only laugh. Only have to.

"It has to be milk and the fake sugar, remember. Awful stuff but better than nothing."

"I get that, Grandma. I get that."

"Glad you're here, my girl. Can't wait to see you." This is an afterthought, and said more matter-of-factly than emotionally, but still I tear up.

The article I was telling lyn about talked about the problems with Redface or the taking on of any face. How when those with power take from those who do not, it is not just taking up space, it's actually violence. Doing this is violence. Letting it happen is violence. Doing nothing.

I stare at my boxes of books, the same boxes that took me so long to pack, now here and I have to undo what took me so long to do. It never seems to end.

lyn

Willow goes to her dad's for dinner and the house is that same quiet it has been all summer. Again. Still. For so long. Night falls faster than yesterday. The trees seem to have started to turn even more. Leaves fall on the sidewalk. I watch them for a second out the basement window. Can almost feel the cold wind all the way down here.

Then I work in a fury. Try to outrun something I can see but am trying to get out of sight. I don't know where in the avoiding my life and loving my work that the art happens but there's this one intersection when things really start flying. Where I only want to can do think of do this. Nothing else but make make make

Vessel 53 is so rough I have to break it apart three times. The clay feels spent and exhausted.

Vessel 55 is a gift. Smooth and easy.

Vessel 56 was fine but I didn't want it to end so I wrecked it on purpose.

The birds cackle outside. Something must have roused them. Their calls make me anxious. I almost go check if they are okay.

June

Before our parents split up, we had a nice maybe even happy little childhood. I mean Renee and Dad were young, super young but that almost seemed normal when I was a kid. A lot of my friends' parents were young, some of my cousins' too.

Renee was also super young looking. Teachers always thought she was our sister and she would giggle like it was the funniest thing. I read once that you kind of stop maturing when you have kids. That makes sense to me. I think Renee was a teenager for a long time. Maybe still is.

But we were happy. We had fun. I remember sitting on her lap while she talked to her siblings. I remember her setting up the sprinkler in the backyard. Sewing costumes with old cut-up clothes. Being there for school things. Making snacks when we got home. She was good.

I know her and Dad split up a few times before they split up for good. I remember him not being around, sometimes for long times, and then coming back and it was the best thing in the world.

One time I went into the basement and all his tools were gone. The tall workbench he made out of an old shed cleared, only one of those small pencils left. I kept it. Treasured it. Put it on my dresser and would only use it super lightly so I didn't have to sharpen it, so it wouldn't get used up. It was red. Painted red on the outside. But then he came back. And we were happy again.

They never screamed, only fought in sinister whispers at the kitchen table while we were upstairs or outside. I remember loud fists hitting placemats, doors slamming, Renee napping for days. That's when I would have to step up and help with lyn. That's when Dad would wake me up before he went to work to tell me he put the milk in our cups in the fridge, so I had to be careful getting it out and pouring it on our cereal. He'd tell me he'd be back when the hands on the clock were straight up and down and to stay in the yard when we got home.

Sometimes he woke us both up and took us to Grandma Genie's for the day. Those were my favourite days. Even though I knew that meant it was a really bad day.

I know Renee didn't have a good childhood. That her dad wasn't the best. She told me he would hit them, but that parents always hit their kids back then. Aunty Dell said he was a mean drunk. She never elaborated.

He died in a farming accident. Renee was the one who found him. That's how she and Dad connected, had both just lost their dads in really bad ways. I was born ten moons later. They really connected.

She had come to the city to get a job and live with her sister. Aunty Dell had a small apartment. After her dad died, Renee stayed back to help care for her mom, but then they got into a fight so Renee hitchhiked the long miles up to the city. Worked crap jobs to stay as long as she could.

That was the story I have always been told. I should ask Aunty Dell to tell me more. Renee wouldn't. Especially not now. Not even if she would talk to me, I doubt she'd tell me the truth.

That's another thing I think of when I think of someone taking another culture, it's at the expense of their own. I mean, Renee's family had their own hardships and challenges, their hero and villain stories. Pick either side—the Quebecois have a long history of fighting mad proud struggle, never mind the Mennos. You ever want a story ask a Menno where they come from, who they come from. They've been kicked out of everywhere and still keep on trucking. I love those stories. One day I'd like to explore them in full because they are also my own. It's a rich, colourful, surprising, exceptional culture in its own right. By taking our stories she is effectively discrediting her own, and those of her actual ancestors. That's sad to me. That's a missed opportunity.

One time I met this African literature scholar and I asked him if he was from Africa. He said, "No way. I'm from Canberra."

"Oh, your people, then?"

"Naw, I just like the stuff."

When I didn't say anything, he added, tone slightly defensive, "I don't come from culture so I am intrigued by it."

We know this is a lie, right? We all come from culture. We're all surrounded by culture all the time. If yours is the dominant culture then that is all you see, but it is still culture. If you don't see it, then you have to question your vantage point.

Renee came from so much. So many stories, such strong people. I wonder why she never thought it was enough.

lyn

Here's where I leap. Where I make connections that only seem obvious to me. Where I tie my project of vessels of the earth together with Circles, also of the earth. Petroforms. Stories written on the land.

Petroform Circles are some of the oldest ruins on the continent. Think Stonehenge but right here in this place. There are several—Montana and the Dakotas and throughout the Canadian prairies but really, they are all over. They're made of stones, are various sizes and scopes, similar to each other but each unique, from a myriad of points in history. There is very little other evidence at many of these sites, which makes archaeologists believe they were mostly used for Ceremony and not for living. Living spaces have garbage or other kinds of waste, and that is always the best way to learn and find dates (carbon, don't you know), but these sites don't typically have much of that, so we don't know how old all of them are. Or they have been in continuous use for generations and on Indigenous land so haven't been poked and prodded for information because they are sacred (like super sacred. The sacredest!) and shouldn't be.

Some have 4 spokes, some have 28.

Some have a circle around them, some don't.

Some have a central cairn, some have cairns at the end, some have neither.

Most are aligned with the summer solstice sunrise and/or sunset. Some are also aligned with other celestial events. Some aren't aligned at all.

Some are believed to be tributes to lost chieftains or leaders. Have great boulders in the middle and lines of rock rippling out.

Some are believed to be an ending place of "vision quests" (quotations because it sounds like academics just guessing).

Some are connected to stories of the little people. (That one sounds more like an actual Indigenous person informed the study.)

Some are believed to be sun lodges as they have 28 poles in a Circle and were temporary structures. This is the meaning that makes the most sense to me, based on what little I know.

> The Medicine Wheel is a modern invention, something
> based on ancient Circles but not quite of them.
> Medicine Wheels typically have
> 4 spokes
> 4 sections within a solid circular surround
> often 4 colours within
> They are seen in art in logos in Indigenous anything
> and sometimes on the ground in one way or another.

It's a beautiful symbol, if only a new one, and has come
to represent the strength in our nations. Not everyone
loves it, but at least it's still a circle.

You can see where I am going with this. Or maybe only I can
right now. See how it all comes together.

Circles. Earth. Back to earth. Back home. Something
like that. Something aligned with the stars and sun and
moon.
A performance.
An active display.
Both

Neither

June

I get to Grandma's right at nine, cardboard cup in hand steaming with her coffee.

She hugs me completely and hangs on for a while longer than she used to. She looks older. It hasn't been that long.

Then she piles frozen bags of berries and fish in my bare arms followed by a light box of knitted things and pushes me out the door in front of her.

"So how has everything been with you?" I finally ask once she's given me the directions to the Friendship Centre, which is good because I always forget home when I return home.

"Oh good, good, you know, keeping busy." She looks out the side window as she sips. I try and catch glimpses of her. But it's like I have to be sneaky about it.

"lyn tells me you're an activist now."

"Oh, that lyn," she chuckles, genuinely chuckles. "I just have a lot of time on my hands, you know. Gotta keep busy. You coming with us?"

"Maybe."

Another one of her pointed looks. I don't even have to turn from the road, I can feel it. "Probably.

"It's good work you're doing." I gesture toward the box in the back seat.

"Oh, that's nothing. Just got no babies to knit for anymore." She sighs, deeply. "Guess I'll have to wait for Josephine at this rate." That's Yoyo's state name.

I was all relaxed, my belly soft, and there she went and sucker punched me.

She insists on going into the Centre even though I could have run in with the stuff. But in she goes like she owns the place. Even chats up the director, a slight lady with a wide smile who seems to know and adore my Grandmother. This is why she had to come in. Grandma Genie never misses an opportunity to receive love.

I show her the house, every room, with ongoing commentary on how we're going to change it. She says nothing until I'm done. Until I sit her on a lawn chair on the small patch of backyard grass and bring her a glass of water. Until she leans back and closes her eyes to the sun, shifting her body toward it, like a cat.

"This business with your mother. Awful stuff." So simple.

"Yeh." It's my turn to sigh deep.

"Must be hard for you. Doing what you're doing. And all that going on."

So simple and yet I have never felt so seen. I choke and nod.

She catches the sudden emotion and looks at me. "Oh, my girl. Don't be sad."

I only nod. "My girl" always sounds just the right way when she says it. "It's okay. I'm just tired." Not a lie.

She pats my hand. Turns back to her sun.

lyn

It's so easy to make a basic vessel. The key things are to make it solid, not too thick so it can cook, even-ish so it doesn't crack, and of course it needs to hold water. But that's it really. There is no reason a vessel can't be super rudimentary. It doesn't have to be smooth, perfectly shaped or ornately designed. These things are not necessary at all. But they are all over the artefacts. Vessels were polished, painted, perfect. Makes you wonder why they did that. Why they played so long they made themselves so good at it. They didn't have to. *Have to* has nothing to do with it.

I sand and smooth today. Slack from the real labour. It's a good job for an off day. I want to curl up on my new used couch and watch something stupid on Netflix with my kid but I am pretty sure I have watched everything stupid on Netflix. And Willow came in only to go out again, to see friends she hasn't seen all summer. She starts school in a few days.

I am not ready for anything.

I am

Shannon and I were going to visit the Circles. Wanted to see each one, check after check on our shared, loving bucket list. I made sample itineraries on my Maps app. They sent me links whenever they saw anything related in the news. I even picked hotels.

From Winnipeg we were going to go southwest first, to the Bighorn site, and of course see the battle site too. I would take pictures, Shannon would drive. I wanted to stand with my love and the tall grass behind us and snap a selfie. Something to find when I'm going through my research. Something to make me smile when I am working later. They really wanted to go into Montana, through Yellowstone and see all the Wild West tourist things (ironically, of course). I wanted to see the Circles in Alberta and finally Moose Mountain, then we could loop back home. We had time booked off. They did. I take time whenever I want to.

I use rocks. Smooth rocks I harvest when I get the clay. All things familiar. I go over the dried vessels, rub off each line with tiny circles. Curve over the lips, run my thumb over my thumbprints. Dust coats my palms where the vessels sit in turn. Fitting perfectly in my hand. Children back where they were born.

The trip stayed in my Calendar, is still on my Maps. Tagged with hearts, a string of them, circled across the territory.

June

After I drive Grandma home, I dig into my class notes. In my new office surrounded by my unpacked boxes. I manage to get the big comfy chair under the east window. It's a great spot. I can see the sun and orange out in the west. The last of the elms and the airport just over my laptop screen.

I nestle in. Into my stories of my ancestors. Women's stories. As awesome and everyday as the sunset.

Buffalo hunters. Sharpshooters. The many who melted down metal to make bullets during the North-West Resistance.

Annie Bannatyne who horsewhipped the naughty Charles Mair in the street on shopping day, humiliated the uppity asshole and inspired a revolution.

Sarah Ballenden—Michif wife of the Chief Factor. She was mistrusted by the newly arriving British women who didn't want to answer up to someone they thought was below them, so they started a rumour that young, beautiful Sarah was cheating on her husband. Reputational warfare. It took a sensational court case for libel, filed by the man she was rumoured to be cheating with, to stop the lies. And though the case was won, Mrs. Ballenden's social standing was never the same.

White folks trying to destroy Michif women, not overtly, not violently—at least not physically, but with whispers, rumours and side-eye. Gossip is a nasty seed, seemingly not sinister, just a question, tiny pieces of sand so small, but wear and wear until they make holes.

The only real way to avoid it is not to participate at all. Not exactly an option for Michif women of that day. Not really an option for any of us, not all the way. Even if we don't go online, we're still in it.

Each one of us is made of stories. Only as good as the ones people remember.

lyn

Willow comes into the room and stresses about school, what I am making for dinner (spaghetti) and how I am making it, the weather. In that order. She sits at the table and I serve her a plate. She serves some news bombs.

"I think I want to take a gap year."
  "Like hell."
  "I want to see the world."
  "Seeing the world is expensive."
  "I can get a job."
  "Of course, you can. Gotta do it though."
  "I think I want to go away for school, too."
  "I knew your aunty was a bad influence."
  "Vancouver's so beautiful. Don't you just love Vancouver?"
  "It's expensive."
  "Is that your answer for everything?!"
  "Not everything but . . . no, you're right, it's the answer for everything."
  "I don't want to get stuck here." She whines this. I don't want to point out to my teenager that she is still whining. But she totally is.

I scoop more sauce (all veggie) on my noodles and add a healthy sprinkle of parmigiano.

I think of four sarcastic things to say, but instead decide on "Yeh, I get that."

June

The carpet in the corner of the dining room is peeled up, one cupboard is ripped off the wall in the kitchen, the lino there also pulled up about two feet. The wall he wants to tear down has a hole, the lath exposed, the broken plaster pooled at the floor.

"What are you doing?" I try not to sound mad.

"Just checking on things." He's slouched on a lawn chair, pulled inside because we don't have anything else, and staring at his phone.

"Checking on how big of a mess you can make?" I go to grab yogurt out of the fridge but the light's off in there. I check behind and it's pulled away from the wall. Not plugged back in.

He infuriatingly does not look up. "Gotta check these things."

"What things?" I squeeze the container a bit too hard and the top opens. White plops all over the counter. What's left of it. Which is when I realize it too is covered in sawdust or just dust. Mess. "Can you get off your phone for a minute?!" Yeh, I sound mad.

He does and sits up. "I'm looking up tools. For the job. We should demo everything this weekend. Your dad said he'd help. And Matt."

"Everything is a mess already!" I huff as I wet a cloth at the sink.

"I was going to clean it up. Give me a minute."

I huff again, is what I do.

"You were right, hey. The carpet is glued on. Like through the whole house."

"Great." I slop at the yogurt.

"What? I thought you'd love to hear that."

"You thought I'd love to hear how hard it's gonna be to take off this gross carpet? How long it'll take? Never mind costing way too much money?"

"No, that you were right." He smiles. That smile he does.

I fix my face. Don't want to smile back. "Don't try to be nice to me. I'm mad."

"What nice? You were right, June."

"Don't sweet-talk me. Not now." I rinse out the cloth. Hang it just so on the tap.

"But you love hearing that so much." He comes up behind me. Gets right up to my ear and whispers hot. "You were right."

I laugh even though I don't want to, and turn to him, even though I have a million things to do.

lyn

I started painting after I couldn't get a poem published. Not even in the high school journal and they literally took anyone and anything. But not mine. So I started doodling in my lined notebooks to fill up the pages with my thoughts. Then I bought unlined ones. I couldn't draw for shit so I bought some paints, little canvases, from the dollar store. I loved painting. I loved when Renee let me use her good stuff. I felt like a little kid in kindergarten again. I painted a lot of daisies. Flowers. Some profiles. Some landscapes. Worked in pencil a bit. Practised for hours. Days. I heard art school needed a portfolio so I got to work. I relished making things. Bathed in it.

June left for school (Ontario). I hung out with Renee a lot. She became my replacement sister again. She was still visiting CokeHead (something about forgiveness) but also dating some guy—Creepy. Not that he was pervy but just because . . . well, who cares, he wasn't important. What's important was that he didn't make her too crazy or try and kill her (that I know of). He was just there. She'd occasionally get annoyed at me that I wasn't nice enough to him but whatever, life was fine. We were close. Renee and me. We went to art things. Did art things. She knew all the great places to get supplies. We were creating and having fun. Seemed so good. For her especially. She was good. Or maybe I only think that because I was living at Dad's. She kept bugging me to come back and live with her, even got a place close to my school saying it was for me (and money was tight for her on her own). But something made me stay. Something in me fought for me, just a little bit (and every time June called, she asked about this specifically, and told me she'd beat me up if I screwed up school). I even got a part-time job. I was so normal. Maybe I was the one who was doing so good.

My sister and I were saving up, going to Europe that summer after I graduated. I couldn't let her down.

But in effect always felt like I was letting Renee down by not moving in with her.

Someone was always let down by me.

I felt bad, wrong, and wrote long unpublishable poems about it. Drew landscapes of the backyard, profiles of the babies, forever in motion, kept trying to perfect hands—my own left one in particular.

Before bed texts:

Willow—I think Dad's gonna buy me that shirt.

Me—I'm so happy for you.

Willow—Thanks! Me too.

Me—How are you doing over there?

Willow—[smiling cat with rainbow shooting out its butt]

Me—Samesies.

Sister—You coming over for this D Day??

Other sister—[Memes. Nothing noteworthy] (Yoyo has such questionable taste.)

Four missed calls

June

When Renee sat us down at the kitchen table, Dad stood by the fridge, and I knew it was different. lyn was still a clued out little kid but I knew. It was fall, or just as good as. The end/ beginning time.

Renee spoke with no emotion at all. Just facts—she got an apart-ment. Dad was going to stay at the duplex. At first, we were both going to go with her. That's when he left the room, when he stormed outside with a slam of the door and paced in the back-yard, smoking.

"Can I stay here with Dad?"

"Junie, no. You should be with me."

"But I want to be here. My house." I didn't say I wanted to be with him. I knew that would hurt her too much.

Then they were both outside for a while. lyn and I watched a rerun of *The Facts of Life*, one with George Clooney in it. Not my favourite *Facts of Life* era.

When they came back in, Dad went right upstairs. Renee sat down and leaned in. She smiled.

"Okay, Junie, you can stay here. lynnie and I will live at the apartment and you can visit."

"Why does she have to go?"

"Well, because she wants to, don't you, lynnie?"

"Wah?!" She didn't look away from the screen. Tootie gave one of her sassy comebacks, there was a laugh track and then no one said anything.

Dad and I lived off of tomato soup and hot dogs. Dad was never home before six. On Fridays lyn would come over or I'd go over there. If we were home, Dad would order us pizza or chicken before he'd go out. He was always tired but still went out. To the bowling alley, to the bar, on a date. If we were at Renee's I had to cook macaroni or grilled cheese. She didn't always go out, but if she was home, she was in her room with ShitFace.

Renee treated me like I was just a silly child for staying, she'd say things like, "When you're done playing house with your dad and you come live here" or "When you're done sulking and come live with us like you belong." But I never wanted to live there. I didn't have a room there. I didn't even have a bed. Neither did lyn. At home I had everything. Except my sister.

If I'm honest, I thought Renee was going to fight me on it, make me come with them, or leave lyn with me. No, if I'm honest I really thought it would make Renee stay and nothing would change.

No, I didn't think she would, only hoped.

But she didn't do any of those things. Instead, she made the ten-year-old make all the decisions on that. Hold all the responsibility. Live with all the guilt.

lyn

Renee wanted to come to Europe with us but couldn't get the funds together. I was going to give her money but Dad talked me out of it. Said we should be young for a while. June planned everything out down to the last detail. I did nothing but pack a bag. We went to Paris, Amsterdam, but stayed mostly in the UK. She left to go back to school and I stayed in Edinburgh.

I had met Daisy.

Daisy was miraculous. Daisy was perfect. Daisy blew my world wide open. We met at a hostel. She was so worldly pretty smart well travelled so pretty. We stayed in bed for days after we met. We'd only go out after the sun went down. We were vampires roaming the cobblestones.

Daisy and I took a ferry to the Orkneys and camped until it got cold (didn't take long). She left me at a bus depot in Glasgow. I thought she was just going to the bathroom. With my last traveller's cheque. The one I signed over and she was going to take to the place. Likely she did.

She had been acting weird for a while.

She had probably been acting weird the whole time.

I don't think she told me many things that were true.

I've never found her on social media (I looked years later). I swear I saw her passport at some point. But you never know.

It's not like I was paying attention.

June said, "I told you so. That chick was not right in the head."

Renee said, "Oh I've been so worried, so worried about you. I am so happy to hear your voice. I have been beside myself with worrying over you. I have been so sad. Creepy left me." (She didn't call him Creepy.)

Dad said, "Go to the bank and see how I can wire you money. You're coming home."

Heartbroken, I was back and missed the start of school—I had to wait until the semester was over. I didn't even have a job. I had missed my great-grandmother's funeral. Dad was sad. Grandma Genie was sad. I was more sad. I pretended to go out and then would sneak back into my room through the window so Kelly wouldn't ask me to babysit.

I partied. I had nothing else to do. Think I was pregnant within the month (not much to do at all). The guy was a friend. Surprisingly this wasn't the worst mistake I ever made in my life.

June

I've always thought of our houses as metaphors for how our life's been going, some sort of symbol for our ever-changing ever-evolving life. Truth is I've always liked it that way. I stayed in Oz and Aotearoa until they kicked me out. I've always gone anywhere else, everywhere else in a heartbeat but for some reason I'm home.

Home.

As long as I've been away, I've never called any other place Home. I mean sometimes I've said it but it's like it's with a different accent. There's home meaning the place I have lived at that moment, where I happened to be sleeping, but it's not really Home, not THE Home. That one sounds a certain way, definitive, with a capital.

I've mostly called the places I've lived "places"—apartments, houses, flats, and I've said I'm home, I'm going home, but it was never Home home. Not really. It was my place. Our place. A place.

Our home right now is more than half broken without even a working fridge. But it's not my real home either.

Home wasn't that mouldy apartment in Kits or any of the many many places we've been, not the too high up one in Sydney or the broken boiler one in Wellington or the bottom half in Auckland.

Home wasn't even our beautiful bright first apartment on Oak Ave. The place we made love in every room, on every surface, on every piece of furniture. The place that looked out over Broadway and almost to the beach beyond it. Not even there.

It wasn't even the house on Barton where Dad and Kelly and all of us lived a whole decade before I moved away, where the little kids were born.

No, if I'm really honest, and I'm trying to be, my real Home is a rented duplex on Berkshire Bay, just past the turn on the down side of the Loop with a backyard that overlooks the footpath then the ditch then the railway tracks. Home is a place where we got used to the overpowering sound of the train four times a day, where lyn and I had matching side by side rooms with matching curtains and bedspreads—hers in pink, mine in purple—and we'd talk to each other through the vent in between our walls when we got sent up there.

Home is the place where I sat against that wall and talked through that vent even after she wasn't there. Where I sat counting the train cars going over that one spot where you could hear them thrump thrump, and remember how when we moved in, my sister and I used to run out to the back fence and wave so the conductor would blow the horn.

Home is where lyn kept her bike because there was no room at the new apartment and we'd still go riding whenever she'd come over. We'd speed down the dirt path into the bush to this place all the kids went to ride in track marked fields, where you could see the abandoned meatpacking plants on the other side of the road. Before the whole area was developed, before all of that was all gone.

Home is where we'd pull the couch from the wall so lyn could play behind it when we'd watch something she thought was too scary, which was almost everything, and where Dad burned any attempt at cookies but we still loved them because they were cookies and we had milk.

Where we'd wait all week for Friday when he'd order pizza or chicken or stop for McDonald's, and I'd meet my sister on the corner and walk her home.

Where I stood on the front stoop and watched my dad pull away with Renee and lyn in the packed Suburban. They all went to their new apartment, and I went back in and watched TV by myself. Dad came home a few hours later with a case of beer for himself and a Slurpee for me, and he sat down and watched *The Simpsons* even though it was still light out and he never sat down when it was still light out.

Home was where I tried my luck and fucked up and wrecked it all and made it worse.

Where I should have kept my mouth shut and gone with her because at least then lyn and I would both be stuck on that couch with the same crazy, but it wouldn't be half as bad because I would take care of her and her and them, all of us. I would have found a way to make it better.

lyn

I never paint anymore. The vessels are unpainted and I've decided to keep them that way. I have missed painting.

I curl the brush around the posterboard, let it drip thick and round. I want it bright and colourful. I want to be able to see it from far away.

Red for power. Dark blue for history. White and black to crisp all the edges.

I change brushes for the letters. Swoop over the W and then the A. Make a round water droplet all around them.

If you flick your wrist just right, it feels like dancing.

My hand aches after. Muscles I haven't used in a while. I step back and smile. Ready.

I drive June and Grandma Genie right up to the Leg and get the signs out of the back. My sister helps our Grandmother out of the car, and gets her hands swatted away, "I'm fine. I'm fine."

I park the car way too far away and jog back to the crowd. I want to find them. I don't want to miss anything. I wish Willow was here but she had so many more important teenager things to do.

I put a protective arm around Grandma, who looks so small today. People around us roar and cheer and boo. Speakers rile us up with information about the world outside of my own selfish head.

It gets so hot. I hold up my sign to block the sun. It's red and black—*You Can't Drink Money.*

Grandma Genie's says *Water Is Life*, blue letters on white curving into a droplet

June's is the same only opposite colours.

In the car home Grandma Genie says, "That was fun. When's the next one?"

June

Grandma makes us come in for food after. I'm not hungry but know better than to say no.

"So, why haven't I seen your handsome husband yet?" she says as soon as I sit down. She's walking slower now. Must be tired.

"Are you okay, Grandma?"

"Oh I'm fine, fine. Just old. I joined one of those tai chi groups, you know. Did that this morning so now, so overdid it, I think. You guys want coffee? Tea?"

lyn: "I'll get it, Grandma. You sit."

She listens but not to be outdone calls, "Get that plate of crackers and cheese out of the fridge. I put it on a plate already."

Then to me: "You have to eat. You don't eat enough."

I smile. Her wrinkled face so kind and distracted with random worries.

"So how's your fancy job?"

"It's fancy. But haven't started yet."

"Important work you're doing. Going to be doing. Did you hear about the lake?"

I'm only confused a minute.

"I shared the post this morning. Did you read it?"

"I didn't look."

"Are you avoiding the Facebook like this one? We have to stay informed. The pollution. Factory farming! It's all so horrible, hey?"

"It is, Grandma."

lyn comes back in with steaming mugs. Tea bags floating to make it dark dark dark just like Grandma Genie taught us to. "Just an activist these days, aren't you, Grandma," my sister says.

"Oh, I am on so many groups these days. All the groups about the lake. We got to save the lake."

lyn and I nod in unison. She plops down and chomps on some crackers, but I think about how I have to get online and start sharing some of my grandmother's posts.

"This nonsense with Renee. Not going away, is it."

There was another this morning. A former colleague, a different one, sent it to me. An op-ed by a prominent filmmaker. All the ways pretendians hurt and take up space. How Renee should give back all her award money to the causes she purported to support. She's not wrong.

The hashtags less active. The heat of it lessened. It was tapering off. Like everyone said it would. Will go away, eventually. Still felt like there was something else I should do. To make it all the way better.

lyn to Grandma: "Have you talked to her at all? In all this?"

"Oh gosh no. I don't think I've talked to your mother since, it was at somebody's funeral. Long ago. She used to call me but it's been years. Probably ashamed, thinking of all this. Why? Don't you talk to her, Juney?"

"I, oh you know. Not since that first article. The one that quoted me."

"Oh, she was mad?"

"You could say that."

"Well, let her be. Chickens coming home to roost and all that."

lyn: "Grandma, did you just quote Malcolm X?"

"Who?"

My sister goes to the bathroom and the room grows quiet. We sit in it. Grandma Genie is getting quieter. Usually she is the first one filling up the space with talk right away. Today she takes a breath or two.

"I am sorry about all this stuff, with Renee."

"Thanks, Grandma. It's not like we're close. Haven't really been in each other's lives for a while."

"That makes me sad. She was a good little mother, Renee. I know she went through some really hard times and all this now," Grandma's bent hand waves. "But she loved you girls. You were her world."

My eyes well up and I swallow. Say nothing.

"I know, she had her challenges, that's for sure. I always thought she was so sad, that one. Like she didn't know how to be happy. Would wreck everything just to prove she didn't deserve it. Your sister's like that, hey?"

She looks off as if studying her plants or the sky outside her window. Finally, says, "We were all so sad there for a time. When you were born, then lynnie soon after. We loved you, oh how we loved you, but we were all still grieving. But you were loved. You were so loved, my girl."

I lean forward and nod. Rub my hands together. Remember the stories of my family. Stories I come from.

She examines the blue in the window, maybe a cloud. "Grief is such a funny thing. It stays with you, you know. It gets to be that it's all you have left."

lyn comes back in. "What's wrong?"

Something clicks in Grandma and she returns to herself, or to my sister: "Oh nothing, my girl, nothing nothing. Eat some cheese. It's too much for me. It'll go bad."

lyn

June's quiet in the car. Loaded up with frozen pickerel on her lap, she looks out the side and says nothing.

Somewhere around the Main Street underpass I finally ask, "You okay?"

"Yeh, I'm fine. I just, I just wish there was something to do. Something I could do."

"Like what?"

"I don't know. Like anything. To make it better."

"To fix it."

"Maybe. But can't I? Isn't there something I can do? There's always an answer."

"I don't know about that . . . I mean, you could do a big social media 'I love Renee she's not a bad person' thing like she wants. Would that make you feel better?"

She gives me one of her fuck off looks. "I think she should apologize and you know, mean it."

"Some people don't apologize. Have you ever known her to apologize? I mean really apologize. She's not going to suddenly grow self-aware and own her shit now."

"But she is guilty. She knows this shit is bullshit. They all do. They can't truly believe—"

"People'll believe anything."

"But it's not right! Anyone else, I would condemn and demand an apology. Her, I didn't really say anything. Didn't get through to her anyway."

I turn down the quiet elm-covered streets of my neighbourhood, our neighbourhood, and sigh. "You said plenty. Have you ever been able to get through to her? I don't think you can. She's too far into it. And it's not your job to get her out. Believe me. It took me so long to learn that but now I know it. I know it so well I can feel it."

"I just think if I say it one way, the right way, then she'll understand."

"Yeh, 'cause that has worked so many times in the past." I am too sharp in my sarcasm (when am I not?). Turn down Garfield. This street has no trees, the whole way, no trees.

"Well, we have to try."

I park in front of her new old brown house. The light on inside. Sigh up and waiting for her. Someone she loves waiting for her when she gets home. "We have tried. We've spent our lives trying."

"We can't just give up."

"Why not?" My voice rises in the anger. Impatience. (Jealousy?) "You do whatever you need to do. I'm not going to tell you what to do, but knowing you, I can tell you for sure, without a doubt, this is not your fault, June. This is not your fault and you have nothing to feel guilty about. Nothing."

It's not all the way dark yet, but the nights are getting longer. Colder. Fall setting in. Winter inevitable.

She gets out and I watch her walk in the door before I pull away.
Drive home slow. Feeling my feelings the whole damn way.

June

Zeke runs down the stairs to greet me. All the lights are on but Sigh's nowhere to be seen.

"Sigh?" I call as Zeke dances. Needing to go out. "Sigh?"

"Up here!"

I find him in the middle of the floor of the second-biggest bedroom. Computer, desk, chair set up. Glass shelves up, toys and lighting perfectly placed inside. Nothing else. His clothes are still in garbage bags. His headphones on as he kills zombies and voices yell along with him in his ears.

"What are you doing?"

"Just playing. What you think?" he says too loud and he quickly motions around before he yelps as an undead comes up behind a building on the screen. Loud moans and calls through his headphones.

"Zeke has to go out." I turn away. My lips a pursed line.

"What?!" Too loud.

"Zeke. Has. To. Go. Out." I stomp down the stairs one by one. Definitely no evening out of my voice.

"I can take him. In a minute," he calls down.

"Never mind," I say under my breath, attaching the leash to a very happy dog with a slightly desperate look.

"What?!"

"I SAID I GOT IT." I slam the door behind me. And regret it immediately, but only because it's such an old door.

Zeke pulls me to the neighbour's fence and lifts his leg. I swear dogs can sigh.

6

good ones

lyn

Texts:

June—you're coming over later right? Is Willow coming?

Dad—they're making it a party? That doesn't sound saf. Need a rid?

Willow—I can't come. I gotta do . . . like anything else in the whole wide world.

Yoyo—Matt's acting strange. I think he's sick of me.

Willow, again—like I'll even clean something here. I'll clean the bathroom. Please don't make me go.

Fifteen missed calls

I didn't want to have an abortion. I would have. Could have. Arguably should have. I completely believe in it as a viable option and that the choice was mine and mine alone.

But I wanted her.

I heard her laughing in my dreams.

I saw her. A funny-looking chubby baby who looked like me. Me but better.

My parents were so young when they had us, I thought I was so much more grown up. Comparatively (awful comparison). I had travelled a bit (one trip), seen a fair bit (lol), gone to school (just started). I thought I was so much more grown up than other people my age.

I wasn't going to ask for anything. But I wanted her. I wasn't even going to tell the dad, and I didn't, at first. At first I only told June.

"You're what?! Are you going to have an abortion?"
    "I don't think so. I think I want to have it."
    "Are you fucking crazy? It will be a human. A human baby, you know."
    "I know but I think, I think I want to."
    "A real live human baby. Like the ones upstairs from you. The ones upstairs who've been crying for years. Those kind."
    "At least I'd have all the hand-me-downs. And stuff. Kelly has loads of stuff."
    "You're fucking crazy."

Dad and Kelly just stared at me.

It was Dad who eventually said: "Well if that's what you want. We're here and we support you."

Kelly said nothing, turned her head and stared at him as he talked. She never said a thing.

Renee was excited. "Oh my god I'm going to be a grandma. Oh my god this is so, oh I'm so happy! We're going to have so much fun, lynnie."

That was the first time I thought it was actually going to be okay. Maybe even good.

My daughter came into the world with June on one side of me, Renee on the other, her dad was there too. She was greeted with love. I forgot how painful everything was before. There was only her. This baby that looked like me. Everyone said it, "She looks just like you," and she was so beautiful. So maybe that meant I was beautiful too. (I really want to say something sarcastic but whatever.)

Willow was about four days old when Renee told me her news. My sister had gone back to school the day before. I had cried when she left, blamed the hormones, and June smiled and said she'd call every day. I had been feeling so alone, hadn't slept. (My kid didn't sleep for a good year.)

But Renee didn't notice my blurry eyes or the screaming baby, she was pacing hands waving so ecstatic. She'd got a job in a gallery. Calgary. Was going to move there right away. It was the best modern gallery in the city. "This is just what I need, lynnie. A fresh start. A job in my field. No more of this dead-end bullshit."

I think I said congratulations. I think Willow spit up or started crying.

I went into my room to change the baby. Cry some more. And worry and hyperventilate a little. I had just registered to go back to school. Renee had promised to babysit because I couldn't afford daycare.

I know at some point she called from the living room. "You got any coffee going? I could use a cup."

I think that was the beginning. Of the end. That moment. My body still soft from giving birth. I felt raw, like I had no skin. But I got mad. So mad. For months, years, I didn't even know what I was mad at. I thought I was mad at my kid's dad for, well, anything. Thought I was mad at my stepmom for being, well, her. Mad at my sister for not being there. It took a while to admit I was mad at the one person I was never allowed to be mad at. And once I admitted that, it was really hard to stop.

June

I love destroying things. When he worked in Wellington, Sigh's job was gutting old buildings. When I could, I'd go with him for D Day and break things for fun. Making a mess on purpose. We're only destroying the kitchen cabinets but it involves a sledgehammer and I'm looking forward to it. I invite lyn and Yoyo to come help. They answered with emojis and exclamation points. Yoyo said she'd bring wine.

Sigh spent way too much money on supplies and materials to start. He's rebuilding his tools collection, he said. He sold a bunch to this guy he was working with so he wouldn't have to haul the big stuff. Only brought one toolbox.

"So what do I do?" Yoyo asks, decked out in spanking-new safety googles, gloves, a bright yellow sledge held like a baseball bat.

"Okay, first you hold it like this." Sigh shows her. "And then you go for the wall here. Here. Not there! Here."

He's very patient is my Sigh.

"Like this? Wow, that was fun. Harder than it looks on TV, hey? I can't . . . it's stuck!"

"You just . . . It's just in the lath there . . . There you go."

"Now what?"

"Now you do it again."

"Again? Like how many times?"

"Until there's no more wall."

"What if, what if the house comes down?"

"It won't come down."

"It might. There's always surprises and things. Walls like, cave in all the time."

"It's not a load-bearing wall."

"Are you sure?"

"Yes, I'm sure."

"Are you sure you're sure? It's an old house. Full of surprises, these old houses."

"Just hit the wall, Yoyo."

"This is not like it is on TV."

Yoyo gave up on the sledge after a few swings. "Think that was my shoulders for the day." lyn does better but not much. I pound down my whole corner of cabinet to hoots of encouragement from my sisters, then huck the broken pieces through the open window and into the backyard.

After a couple of hours of doing mostly nothing, Yoyo says, "This goes much faster on TV. Anyone want a Starbucks?" Sigh and Matt were grunting the very old stove out the back, and Dad was overseeing the delivery of the new stuff in the front. Sigh's even got Matt talking. Sigh can get anyone talking.

Yoyo comes back with coffees and we sit on the floor looking out the dining room window. Back lane and the backs of houses. The changing leaves bright in the sun.

Yo: "This is nice."

Me: "I'd love to make this window patio doors."

"Oh yeh, with a deck out in the back!"

"One day."

"Or you could move the kitchen in here. More light here."

"Naw, that'll be too much hassle. To move the appliances and stuff."

"Just get them to do it. They're strong men."

"No, I mean the hookup. Electrical. Water."

"You got a couple outlets right there." Yo points at the regular outlet on the wall.

lyn: "You need a special hookup, Yoyo. How did you survive Dad and not learn anything about building stuff? We never heard the end of it."

"Oh, I was never interested in that stuff. Besides, he had Riel."

"Oh!" lyn and I say in unison, thinking of our baby brother.

Me: "Yeh, I guess we were pretty unisex to him."

lyn: "Mediocre boy stand-ins until he got his real one."

Me: "Poor us, neglected girl children."

Dad walking back inside: "What's this now?"

lyn and I look at each other: "Nothing, Daddy."

"Oh shit, they're calling me Daddy. I must be in trouble now."

lyn

Night all the way here and I'm not even tired. Willow was out when I got home but the bathroom was quickly wiped down and sprayed with room spray.

I am restless,

Where are you?

Friend's

When are you coming home?

Hour?

I should get you. It's dark.

It's three blocks. I'll text you when I leave.

My kid must have been annoyed, to text in full sentences.

The street is quiet no one to spy on. I breathe into the evening and try and feel. My sore arms from work. Will ache tomorrow.

My legs too, from hoisting things into the back. Garbage right into the bin. June was so happy. And was right. It was fun.

But now I'm tired, weepy, vulnerable.

They say every time you remember something you remember it differently. You relive it, go through it all again. Sometimes you can do this and heal. Sometimes it just feels like you're starting at the beginning again. Apparently, it's not the beginning, it's progress, always progress, however incremental. (I call bullshit.) Only feels the same.

A spiral by nature is not a circle, it moves different. Makes a path. Forward maybe.

Bigger, wider, anyway.

A therapist asked me once, "What do you want from Renee?" and right away I said, "I just want her to be normal." And they gave me this look, one of those really good therapist looks that make you understand you're being silly. Unrealistic. Stupid. Unfair to both of us. All of us, really.

Then they added the extra sucker punch by asking, "How would you define normal?"

Aware of their point, I indulged anyway. "Attentive, affectionate, mature, maternal . . ."

"So, like a mom from a TV show."

"Well, yeh, and no. She can be human. Go poop and stuff." I think I was actually pouting.

"So not so much normal as perfect."

But I can be so obstinate. "Perfect gets a bad rap. It's not like you have to be perfect, only strive to be perfect. You might not get there but you'll get close. Closer, anyway."

"How do you know she wasn't trying to be perfect?"

"Well, pshha, if she did, she didn't get anywhere close."

"Do any of us?"

June

I go to the nearly empty university a couple of days before classes start. Teachers are teachers everywhere and don't go in until they absolutely have to. That's not to say we're not doing a bunch of work on our own all the time, but that's in the comfort of our own homes. Classrooms can feel like a ball and chain when you always have to be there at a certain time for a certain day. It's exhausting. I love it but it's exhausting.

I love the freedom of working from home more. I used to love it all summer but then I got used to it all year. I love doing my laundry on what would be coffee breaks. I love wearing sweatpants and checking my email while my online classes work in small groups. I love it when no one is watching me. Mandated office hours and actually in-the-office time and in-person classes feel harder now.

I'm being a little baby really. I only have two in-person classes and am on two committees that will probably have online meetings. I have office hours but I'll probably only have to be here three days a week, and in all honestly, with my house in chaos for who knows how long, I'll probably work here as much as I can for a while yet. Just as long as it's my choice and not a have-to.

It's a super gentle schedule to start. I won't even start any thesis advising until next year. This year is all about settling in and buttering me up. Not that it will be easy, but the perception of easy. They're giving me enough rope, really. Truly, I need to be working my ass off. I should be publishing and writing constantly. They will want to see what I can do and how I prove myself. This is only tenure *track*. It's a path. I've got to walk it. I am not there yet.

I do have a pretty decent publishing record. Better than most, not as great as some. Maybe only better than some. My goals are to start with a thorough lit review of what they have in the library and uni records and at least two new chapter/articles this year. Hopefully I can also build a synopsis and create a plan for a book. If I am super lucky, I can even sell the idea or get an agent to sell it. That's pie in the sky territory though. I'd be happy with a couple of articles and a consistent writing schedule. It looks like I'll have two days to write but really, between all the committees, students, admin, that time tends to get eaten up. It's so easy to keep occupied with the business of things. So much that you stop doing what you're supposed to. Writing always gets pushed away. Always.

My office is beautiful. I probably only love it because it's new to me, but the window is big and I feel happy in it. My first by myself all the time office.

It really is a piece of shit. This whole uni is a series of hastily constructed buildings smooshed together making one big hastily built building. This office is no exception but at least it has a window. The folks across the hall are not so lucky, though a couple overlook a little atrium. I remember going in there as an undergrad and studying among the plants some poor admin was trying to keep alive. They have since given up and the small outside space is plantless. The old benches are the same though.

My desk is easily from the seventies. The built-in shelves that line both walls just standard brown wall shelves. An old landline covered in dust. Beige blinds and a view of the bus depot. The window opens, thankfully. I remember having a meeting with a prof in one of these offices once. I wonder which. I wonder if it was this one.

lyn

Morning texts:

Grandma Genie—when's the next protest? [laughing emoji] (Only one?!)

Aunty Dell—alright. You win. I am coming over for dinner. What day works?

Dad—How'd you like all the demo? Ready to come work for me? Haha (I don't think he knows about lols.)

Willow—I need new shoes.

Big sister—I think I made a mistake.

I pick up the phone for this last one:
    Me: "No you didn't."
    June: "Yes I did."
    Me: "You're just nervous."
    June: "I think you mean triggered."
    Me: "That's just Winnipeg."

June

I sifted through my DMs, deleted a bunch from reporters, and Renee's. Felt bad about it but couldn't deal with it right now and needed to check there wasn't anything I needed to know for school. I stop when I see his name, sandwiched between two reporters from conservative media:

Hey, I hope you're doing ok.

I click on his photo before I can even think on it. His face gets bigger, both his dogs in the frame. The beautiful goldens.

He's posted a few of the current goings-on but nothing personal. He wouldn't. He never does.

I dive into an article about protesters in Labrador occupying a dam and try and forget about him specifically. I have been out of the loop. Need to catch up.

Once I'm thoroughly distracted with the fucked-up state of the world, and have stopped shaking, I go in and delete his message. Not that Sigh would ever go into my stuff, or that there was anything untoward to see, but I like to do that, delete the messages, so I don't go back and obsess. So they don't exist anymore. I don't even think about it anymore, it's like a reflex. I know it makes it look worse than it is.

Tomorrow, we will bring my books and go to the Greek place to drink beer and eat feta until we're gassy. But now I will wander the old halls, try to find where my classes are. Try and find them without asking anybody. Get lost a bit but keep wandering. That's how I always get my bearings, by getting lost.

Then I walk home. To my place and my husband.

I take the long way. It's a nice day, I tell myself.

I only want to walk a little longer in the nice day.

lyn

Renee came home from Calgary after a few months. She never said she was fired but I got that impression. She started volunteering at some galleries downtown, in the Exchange. Couldn't find another job and refused to "go backwards" and pick up an old one. She started talking about us all getting a place together.

She didn't visit until she'd been home a week. Willow was crawling and Renee didn't even look exclaim realize how amazing my child was. I asked her if she wanted to babysit and she made excuses.

It hadn't been long, but everything about Renee looked different. Sounded different. The way she talked shit about everyone, always with this judgmental tone, her siblings, my kid's dad, my own dad. Everyone but herself.

She wore her hair in a headscarf. Wrapped in a geometric print. So many colours. Coiled like a turban.

She asked me what I was working on.
  "Um, parenthood? I have a baby."
  "That's no excuse. If you're an artist you have to create. I started belly dancing when I was pregnant with you."

"Well, I was thinking of going to school but can't really afford daycare."

"Get Kelly to do it. What else is she doing?"

"Kelly works."

"Since when?"

"Um, forever."

"She just seems the type to milk it for all it's worth."

I didn't want to ask more. What her type could be or why (cough cough racism cough).

"If you could watch her . . ."

"Oh no I couldn't possibly. I don't even know how long I'm going to be in town. Really don't like the prospect of another winter. My joints have been killing me lately." (She was like mid-thirties!) (Okay, I shouldn't make fun, I have old person pain now too.)

She left a few weeks later. Said goodbye with a phone call. Somewhere on the West Coast. I didn't ask where.

June

Sigh turns down the music as I creak down the stairs. This is our compromise. Something one counsellor told us to do. Sigh likes music on all the time and I need quiet, especially in the mornings. Counsellor said maybe if he turned it down, maybe if I had a say in what he played. That last part's never happened, but he does turn it down.

"Hey! Going in again?"

"I want to set up my office some more. You're making progress!" I can be supportive. The glued carpet now in strips, still stuck to the floor.

He points. "This is oak under here!"

"Really? Can you save it?"

"Naw. I have to basically chisel this stuff off."

"What a waste!"

"No kidding!"

"Okay. Love you . . ." I'm lingering.

"Love you too."

"Don't start any more projects until the kitchen is all the way done, please." Didn't sound nagging at all.

"I won't."

"I mean, I know you want to change everything. I do too but we should do one thing at a time."

"Yes dear."

"I mean it!" Gentle, gentle.

"Don't worry."

"I never worry!" I'm so cheery even my voice is smiling.

"You always worry."

"I love you."

"Go to work already."

lyn

I stopped answering when she called. I didn't return voicemails. It took her a few months to notice. Then she called and called.

I answered on an unknown number (like a total amateur).

"Oh so you're avoiding me and now I finally hear your voice."

"Renee?"

"Yes, has it been so long? So tell me, what's with the spoiled brat routine?"

Willow was tottering around and I was trying to get ready for the day. Get the baby in the stroller, distract her with my house keys.

"I'm not trying to act like a brat, Renee."

"Well, you're acting pretty ungrateful after all I've done for you."

"I've just been busy. I . . ." She didn't interrupt. I didn't say anything. Willow squealed and made the keys go and go.

"Busy? Likely story. What's going on? Is that Kelly putting you up to this?"

"No, I . . ." I wanted to tell her about what I was doing. Back in school. My baby was walking. I felt kind of great to be getting by. But she never asked.

Then she was crying: "I never raised you to be so cruel."

And I blubbered: "I'm not trying to be cruel. I—"

Shrill screaming: "You're not going to stop me from seeing my grandchild!" She hung up.

I didn't know what I was going to say before she interrupted me.

After that, I wasn't avoiding her so much as I was trying to leave it. Trying to let it all just settle down. That's how it started. Just a settling down.

That's when the messages started. On my voicemail.

Anger: "How could you do this to me? How could you? After all I've done."

Seething: "I see through you. I know what you're doing and I won't let you do it. Oh no. I am talking to a lawyer. You can't stop me from seeing my granddaughter."

Hyperventilating kind of crying: "Oh please, lynnie lyn, please my girl please talk to me."

Seemingly level: "This is the last time I am going to call. I give up. I give up. You win. You have taught me my lesson. I get it. I said one wrong thing. I'm sorry so sorry that I got too involved. It's just 'cause I love you. My one great fault. I love you guys so much. All of you. But don't worry, I won't call anymore."

She still called. But less often.

I was waiting for a nice message. A "hey how you doing?" kind of message. I still think I would have responded to a nice message. But it never came.

And, eventually, she did stop.

June

I'm staring out the window over my laptop screen contemplating a late afternoon coffee when someone knocks on my open door. I figure it's a student but when I turn it's an older white lady with a big smile, someone I've only ever seen online at staff meetings. It's always strange to see a whole body where you used to only see a head.

"Hello! Juniper! I've been meaning to come by. How are you settling in?"

"Not bad, Janice. How are you?"

"Oh it's all the same for me after a while. Have I told you I am so glad they hired you? So glad. It's about time the dean got off her ass and added some real colour to the place."

I breathe in. Smile awkwardly.

"I also wanted to tell you I heard about that mess with your mother. So sad. So very sad."

I make a non-committal sound.

"You hear about this so much these days! So many people are being called out, it's all over."

My sore throat tightens. I really need a coffee. "Yes, it's a real problem."

"I'm sure you heard, the Fine Arts Department over there had to let her go. Well, not renew her contract. That's what I heard. She was only on contract. But they had no choice. None of us do, really. You won't believe the hoops we have to go through nowadays. The administration has created a committee."

Knowing something of the profound effort it takes to get academics to sit on yet another committee, I express something of an "Ohh!"

She goes on: "There are more than a few here who have never shown any sort of cards, so I really do wonder what will happen."

If she wasn't blocking the door, I'd run away.

"At least you're safe with your *Métis* card, eh? We had to check that, you know. When we hired you. I think we're going to have to check everyone from here on in."

My eyes glaze over. "Well, it's ID like any other. Most places require things like—"

"To think, all this fuss . . ." She shakes her head.

I can feel my smile fade and don't even bother to change my face. It's not that I blame them for checking. Everyone should be checking all the time, or creating functional systems that can consider all the different colonial fuckery that has been imposed upon Indigenous identity. To be clear, I am resentful of this burden, another one, on us, the ones who didn't do anything. The burden is on us rather than them, the ones who (1) lied their pants off and (2) believed their shit. The fact that I have to sit here and be a sounding board for this basically-a-stranger's feelings.

"I was such a fan of your mother's work, you know. What a shame."

I say nothing. This is something else I hate. White people's versions of NDN are always so palatable to white people. No one ever wonders about why though.

"Oh well, I'm glad you're all settled in. You let me know if you need anything."

And just when I think I am rid of her, she turns back to me: "Oh and Juniper, you remind me next week sometime, we have some special students. They are so special and work so hard, but they're from up north, you see, and seem to need some extra . . . care and attention, just to keep them on track. I thought you'd be the perfect person to do that. What do you think?"

There is always the extra work. I don't mind it. I consider it my job to help out those coming after me. I only wish my non-Indigenous colleagues would also have something extra to do. "Sure, Janice, I'll email you early next week and we'll set something up."

"Oh, good on you. Thank you, Juniper. I knew you were one of the good ones."

lyn

Midday texts:

Willow—I think I am going to do bio instead of chem. Thoughts?

Yoyo—Do you think Matt is right for me?

Aunty Dell—what should I bring?

Grandma Genie—I signed you up for an art thing

About an hour later I think on this more and go: What art thing?

Some people are doing an art thing.

What?!

When Grandma doesn't reply, I call. Her voice exasperated, the background noisy. "Yes, my dear, what is it?"

"What is this art thing?"

"Some community organization. Their art teacher dropped out and they needed an art teacher and I thought you're an art teacher." She's out of breath. Walking fast.

"Who? And when?"

"I don't remember the name. I posted something about what they're doing so you can look at that. It's with the river."

So many questions. "Um. When?"

"Tomorrow."

"Tomorrow!"

"Yes. Can you get me around eleven? Maybe eleven thirty. It's not until lunchtime but I'm making bannock and will need help carrying it all out."

"What?!"

"Gotta go, honey. We're lapping around the mall and I'm running out of breath."

As she hangs up, I can hear her starting up again, a "So anyway" to her fellow walkers, as if I had interrupted her.

I get Willow to look up the post so I know the name and place at least. I think of things I can do, mull supplies and Teachings for a while. Over dinner and dishes, my daughter and I list the pros and cons of studying biology versus chemistry at the high school level, specifically for someone who has no interest in either. It's a spirited debated for which I play the devil's advocate with great aplomb for the rest of the evening.

My kid is so much like my sister.

I waited it out. Wanted to. Took care of Willow. Went to school. Made art.

June was still talking to her. I found out things here and there.
Renee went to Toronto at some point. Back to Toronto. Didn't
know why, but did ask:

"You going to see her?"

"Probably at some point."

"Is she doing okay?"

"Are *you*?"

"I just want her to apologize."

"Good luck with that."

Something so small sometimes feels so big.

June

I'm sitting out on the porch when Dad comes out. I look up from my book, and he is covered white with dust.

"How goes the drywall?"

"Man, I really hate drywall."

"By the looks of it, it doesn't like you much either."

"Har" is all he says. I glance in the window and see Sigh mixing the mud and slapping it over the seams. I do love watching him work.

"This is a good porch." Dad settles into Sigh's chair. "Reminds me of the brown house porch. Remember the brown house?"

lyn's been telling me about this, about Dad's memory lane. I smirk at it. "Of course I remember the brown house, Dad. I was a teenager when they sold it."

"Margaret should have never sold that house." He's shaking his head over real estate sold years ago. "Grandpa Mac built that porch. It was like this. My dad and uncles helped him. Man, that was a good day. My dad and uncles got all drunk and Grandpa Mac was such a worker, hey? Didn't like that." He chuckles and looks off, to the neighbours cutting the grass, the sky, who knows. I don't want to interrupt, only smile at his smile.

"I bet," just to make sure he knows I'm listening.

He laughs. "That was a good summer. Mom was so happy that summer. That was the summer before."

Ah, I think but don't say. Before his dad died. That sad big thing that changed everything. There's always a before.

I nod but he doesn't continue.

"Hey Dad, can I ask you something?"

"Uh-oh."

"What do you think about all this Renee stuff?"

He leans back, sighs. "Well, I think she's pretty heartless, I'll give her that." This is the closest Dad gets to speaking bad about Renee. My dad's story being used as her own. A particularly sharp violation. But still, he's always gone by the rule of not talking shit about her in front of us. As old as we are he still does this.

"Yeh," I sigh. "I wish I could like, understand, you know?"

"Well, she's not exactly all there anymore, hey?"

"What?!"

"I mean, neither of us were, hey. The way we both lost our dads like that. Maybe she's still grieving like that. Some people never stop. Your Grandma was sad for years after my dad died. I was too, took me years get over that. If I ever did."

"Yeh."

He checks himself. "But you! You were a gift, Juney. Best thing to happen in the whole world."

"You don't have to say that, Dad."

"I know. But I mean it." He winks at me.

"Thanks."

"I always thought she got angry. Thought it was because of me for a long time, but then realized she was just angry. I mean

I was far from perfect, but some people get like that when they're hurting, always mad at someone. Aunty Margaret was like that, but with everybody."

"Yeh, I remember I was always scared of her. She was mean. Well not mean, more like tough?"

"Naw, she was mean. Mean and mad. She the maddest person I had ever met, until Renee got all mad. But Renee wasn't like that when we were kids. When we had you guys. She loved you guys and was a really great mom, all things considered. She did good. But she didn't stay that way. She was too hurt, I guess."

"Do you think something happened, or was it just what happened before?"

"Who knows? I'd be the last to know. Haven't really talked to her since you were young. When she started with that one guy, she stopped talking to me altogether. Or maybe 'cause you two were old enough to relay any messages, she didn't have to talk to me."

"I remember that. She was with CokeHead then."

"Yeh, he was something, that guy."

"Piece of work. Uncle John knew him, hey? In prison."

"Doesn't surprise me. Sadly."

"Yeh, that was all a very sad thing. I felt for her during all that."

"She knew how to pick 'em, hey?"

He is so thoughtful, eyes stuck on the sky. And I think of what my words could mean to him: "I didn't mean, Dad . . ."

"Naw naw," he shakes it off. "I do think him and that other one, I don't think they were good to her."

"They were assholes, Dad. Wastes of space."

"Well, that's not her fault, hey?" He turns to me. Looking at me long.

"It's good you can defend her."

"Maybe." He turns away again. "Kelly always thought she was crazy. Borderline, she called it. I looked it up once, it means you can't control what you do or your emotions or something. Extreme, that's it. Those people are extreme in how they deal with things."

"She is that."

"I don't know if that's what she is. I still remember that little kid, hey? With her chubby cheeks and curly blond hair. Man, she was a looker! Don't know how I ever got up the courage to talk to her."

"At Kildonan Park Pool . . ." I start the story in singsong. Not that I've heard it in years.

"Yeh, if you can believe. Me wearing my dad's old T-shirt 'cause I was so shy. Never went to the pool without a shirt on. She was wearing a red bikini. Sitting in the shade reading a magazine. I asked her for the time."

"Slick."

"Hey, it worked, didn't it?"

"Sure did."

"You were born not even a year later."

"Meant to be," I finish.

"Sure was." He looks off, into somewhere. "We were so young, hey? I think too young to do you two any good. I feel bad about that. That we didn't give you what you needed."

"Dad." I look at him, even though he doesn't look back. "You did the best you could."

"I know, Juney. But so did she, hey? I don't think she ever had a chance to grow up. Not all the way. I feel bad for her, really."

I nod. I don't know if it's in agreement or only acknowledgement, but it feels like the right thing to do.

We're quiet for a long time. Until some sort of internal clock seems to click and he's tired of sitting. He gets up and pats my shoulder as he goes. "I'm sorry all this is happening to you guys."

"Me too, Dad. I'm sorry for you, too."

"Hey, I'm tough. I'll be fine."

"Me too, hey."

"Yeh." He smiles down at me. "You come by that honestly, you know."

lyn

I'm late getting Grandma so she's waiting on the bench outside her building. Two big silver trays of warm bannock I take from her lap but still feel shame.

I pick these up again after I park the car. After she gets out and walks ahead to greet the people. She seems to know them or they know her. She seems so at home as they offer her a lawn chair. (I forgot lawn chairs.)

A group of mid-grades squirm around in the grass as I mutter through some Teachings I know, in prep of an art exercise I do. I feel rusty and nervous, but Grandma is beaming at me. I tell a Creation story. In a world covered in water, Sky Woman falls to the back of a turtle. Trapped with few friends, she sends them down to find earth. And it is Otter, normal, small, kind of meek Otter, who is the only one who dove far enough to bring back a scoop of dark wet earth. The one no one thought would ever be a hero. Underestimated Otter.

From the Teachings I get the kids (students) to play with clay. Some make otters, others turtles. This one quiet kid at the back makes a likeness of a tall woman riding a turtle astride. Her long hair flowing behind her.

I make arrangements with the organizers to fire the pieces, bring them back next week so the students (babies) can paint them.

Grandma keeps beaming.

In the car, after the underpass and way down the road, she finally says, "You're good at that. You should do that all the time."

"I feel more tired than I have in months."

"It's a good tired though," she sighs. "You know, I spent a good part of my life being sad, being in mourning. Began to be a big waste of time, if you ask me. That's tiresome!"

My Grandmother only married the one time. Like most tragedies like that, it's always looming and unsaid. Except now she's saying it. I cock an eyebrow and smirk gently (can one gently smirk?).

"It's okay to be sad, sure, but it gets boring, if you ask me. I mean, I love my Joseph and miss him terribly to this day, but I spent too long being stupid with that."

I try. "Grandma, you were mourning. And you were young."

"I was old enough to know better! But I was so worried about your dad, then he and Renee had your sister so I was worried about all them. Your Mamere Annie, oh she was so sad. We were all so sad."

I nod. Don't take my eyes off the road.

"You know what it was? It wasn't just sad. I was in shock and it was awful, but after a while it wasn't sadness, I was scared. That's what it was. I mean, I got married when I was eighteen, had your dad, was a wife. Didn't know anything different. Didn't want to be anything different. I was so scared.

"But then I got out there, went back to work. Got us all out of that sad house. I needed to go, be on my own. And I did it. I was good at it. Could have knocked me over with a feather the day I realized I was okay. Successful, in that. Did what I set out to do and was even pretty good at it."

I can feel her eyes on me. "You're okay too, I think. I don't think you know it yet, but you're okay, my girl. Even in all this, this fucking bullshit."

"Grandma!"

"What, I can swear! I'm good at that, too."

7

this vessel

June

I go on my socials a little longer these days. Still not commenting, still pretending I'm not there. As if I am not checking a million times a day.

They're still talking about Renee but not as much. She hasn't made a statement. That original reporter posted that he got a cease and desist from her lawyer but that's all he said. He didn't retract anything.

It's only slander if it's proven untrue.

I hang out on Grandma Genie's page awhile. Long-winded status updates, a couple of quote boxes framed with stylized florals, a selfie profile pic a little too close to her nose and angling up. She's been posting a lot about the lake, helping with a fundraiser, informing. This all fills me with a deep love and I want to post a comment, but I don't want anyone to know I'm here. I can't hold back a like.

His name pops up in one of her articles about the bacteria-killing algae caused by factory farming. He had been quoted. A good quote. His perfect words. This, too, fills me up. Gratitude.

I bring up his picture. His beautiful face and two dogs.

Me—Hey. How are you?

The dots pop up right away. His dots. There is a knowing in me. A familiar feeling I sink into.

Him—Hi! How are YOU? I have been thinking of you.

I can see his face. The way it lights up when he sees me in a way even I can't ignore. My lips soften, the way they do when I know I am admired. Like sunshine. I close my eyes, bask in it a minute.

I'm ok. Settled in. All good.

I mean with this Renee stuff, duh?

He's the kind of person that cuts through bullshit but in that good way. The way that doesn't feel pushy, only caring.

I'm fine totally not freaking out.

Sounds like you

lol

Your statement was good. Better than I could have done.

Thanks.

And when I write nothing else, he goes: You did all you could, you know.

Something I have heard a hundred times, from people who love me, from myself, but still.

Thanks for saying that.

I miss you.

Followed up too quick with: Staff meetings are boring now. They make us come in person and totally cheap out on the muffins. These assholes!

I smile. Cling on to the "miss you" awhile.

Him—You going to the conference next month? I am present-
ing that paper. You should come.

There is another knowing. I hesitate. I start and stop and start
again. Don't think so. I didn't apply for the leave. Prolly too late now.

A beat, and then his Prolly.

An inside joke between us. Something that when explained
doesn't even sound funny. But also,

Something in the things we've said. And not said. The gentle
turning down. An invitation regretted. Opportunity not taken.
The mood shifts. You can feel it even in the miles between us.
Maybe it had changed already. Maybe it will only keep changing.

Him—I should run. Take care, Stranger.
Me—You too.

All our inside jokes. Or not even a joke, just a something inside.
The pattern of our interaction. Familiar, warm, lovely. He admires
me. An admirer. I admire him, too.

Sigh doesn't admire me. Admiration is superficial thus unneces-
sary, or maybe just unretainable, in marriage.

lyn

Vessels are for carrying
water food belongings it is
what they are
made for

I was never good enough for Shannon. That's the real story. I
don't know who was more critical scared unhappy. Miserable.
They moved out three whole times, almost did—dozens of,
threatened to, but always came back. Always, except for once.

The pattern was the same: we started strong, centred each other.
I centred them. Then life happened. I stopped overfunctioning,
they started, they stopped. For me it felt comfortable, normal-
izing, easy. For them it sounded like it was death. They needed
whatever I wasn't giving. I needed peace. I fought for it (apparently not the way to go about getting it) and when I fought, they
wanted to leave.

Distance grew in silence intervals widened. They worked late I
worked late I worked early someone "fell asleep" on the couch.
Avoided. I was so afraid I held my shoulders up my torso ridged
bracing my whole body

then they'd leave and I'd be shocked all over

They always said they were going to leave, then they did. I only ever said I wanted them to stay.

> it is said women
> are water
> carriers but
> don't we all
> carry water?

When I met them, I had been in therapy for years. Thought I was so grown up because I could name my ailments, recite them along with my astrological sign and favourite foods:

> I cycle through depression and anxiety
> I have a major fear of abandonment
> I am scrappy and can make a fight out of almost
> anything
> no really, anything
> codependent disorganized attachment
> overfunctioner
> aquarius
> butter chicken with navratan and lots of naan
> I was so proud of knowing myself
> these mines I learned to
> walk around to
> avoid

we feel it in our water water is what we are made of water is one
of the four elements water represents emotion emotion flows
through us as sure as energy breath love life breath love life
blood love love love

       never occurred to me I could befriend them
       those things that list my stuff
       never even thought I could help them
       heal
       only knew of
       them
       believed that
       was enough
       but I should have known I was
       never enough

vessels are for holding
literal sustenance
things that sustain us within
a thing that sustains

June

There is a smell in the bathroom I think is mould. The bed still isn't set up and main floor is a wasteland but at least it smells like fresh paint.

Sigh is out getting more supplies, more things to put on the line of credit.

I get up from my computer and pull my old running shoes out of a still unpacked box. Zeke is delighted by this turn of events.

There are three new deliveries in the spare room. Boxes all the same size. I kick them and they are light. More toys. Also on the line of credit.

When walking isn't enough, I start to run, just slow. My dog looks up with sheer glee, immediately matches my pace, and we bound around the corner. lyn's house comes into view. My sister and another person sit on the stoop, shaded in the evening light.

"What are you doing?"
    "What do you mean, what I am doing? I'm jogging."
    "You hate jogging."

"I like to jog sometimes."

"When times?"

"When I'm . . . restless I guess."

Aunty Dell stands up to hug me: "Oh stop bugging the woman. Come here, you. I haven't seen you in what, a year? Two?"

"I don't even know. How are you?"

"You know, same old same old. How's the new job?"

"Okay. Surviving." I shrug. Zeke finds a bush he likes.

"Best you can hope for. They're not giving you any grief about all this stuff with Renee?"

"No, not too bad."

"You talked to her?"

Before I can answer, lyn gets up. "Oh hell, if we're going to talk about that, I'm going to open that wine you brought. Pull up a stoop, sweaty arse."

I sit down. "No, I haven't spoken to her since . . ."

"Since it all came out?"

I nod.

"How'd she take it?"

I shrug.

"That good, eh?"

"I don't think she was doing great before."

"She never really done too great. Poor Rennie."

lyn comes back with fingers clinging around three plastic tumblers and a bottle under her arm. Sits on the grass in front of us.

I sip quick. Zeke leans into me. I think too long, not long enough. "When we were kids, she was depressed, right?"

lyn laughs. "Uh duh, yeh."

Aunty: "Depressed? Hell yah. We're all depressed. All us kids. Rennie got a little more I think though, sure. She had her bad patches."

"Was she ever like, diagnosed with anything?"

"Not back then. But now, I don't know. I haven't talked to her in what, ten years? Maybe more? Don't think she'll be taking my phone calls now. Not that she would have before."

"I've been worried about her. That something's really wrong with her. I've been trying to, you know, cope with her, but it's getting harder."

"They say that. That these things get worse with age. If you don't deal with 'em, you know. But really, she'd never let you help her even if there was. We weren't built that way."

I sigh.

lyn refills my glass with an arched eyebrow. I had drunk it too fast.

Aunty: "I always thought she had the PTSD or what do you call it C-PTSD, the longer one. After my dad, how he died. She was the one who found him, eh?"

I look at my sister. "Yeh, we knew that."

lyn: "She'd always tell us about it."

"Really? Fucking Rennie. No business telling kids about that. That's why I think PTSD sometimes. If you read on it, sure sounds like her."

"Maybe."

lyn: "I don't think it matters, you know. I mean, personally it doesn't matter to me what she is. She's mean. That's all that matters."

"But if she's sick," I try.

"She wouldn't ever admit it if she was. It wouldn't change anything anyway. She'll just go on to another lie or man or whatever she does now. Won't change anything."

"Maybe." But I also think, "Or?"

Aunty: "Sadly I think lynnie's right, hon. I don't think my sister could face that."

"Then how do we help her? Do we just stay away? Forever?"

"That's what she seems to be asking."

"But that's not right."

"Nothing ever is."

I stare at the glass in my hands, cradle it, don't want to gulp this one down too. But do.

Aunty Dell changes the subject. An uncle's heart condition, all the cousin gossip, everyone sounding so many years older than the last time I heard about them. "I'm hoping we can get through the year without another funeral. Tired of those."

"I thought that's where you picked up the chicks." I laugh, an old joke she told us once. Completely scandalized Sigh at the time.

"Not in Menno land! Christ, those ladies are so closeted, I'd need to bring a crowbar to get them out of there."

My sister and I burst out laughing so hard that lyn snorts, so we laugh at that.

"What?!" Aunty keeps going. "It's true. They got padlocks on them fuckers."

lyn wipes her wet eyes with her palms. "Ah heck, my aunty. They're going to excommunicate you one day."

"Excommunicate this." She slaps the side of her butt. "Naw, that's a Catholic thing. Mennos'll just talk about you behind your back and shun you until you feel uncomfortable and leave."

Me: "So, like white people."

"Careful, don't tell them that. They think they're the persecuted ones."

"So, like white people." I giggle. So does my sister.

Aunty Dell is the one laughing too hard now. I'm glad for it. I can see why lyn likes it. This lightening of things.

lyn

Yo—I need a break. A night out. Summer's almost over. We should
have a fire!

Grandma Genie—Proud of you. [long line of every colour heart]
(Maybe she does know.)

Willow—READ THIS [attached article]

Of course I ignore it. Stick my hands in soft cool clay.

But she beeps another—do it

it's good!

I mean it

You better

Mother!

So I click on it and she's right,

it's that old gallery owner I used to know, the one I warned about Renee years ago. She said that I did that, that June has been working tirelessly, both of us worked so hard, were genuine in our community connections, how we are not to blame.

It was so beautiful I cried.

My kid comes downstairs to see me (something she never does). "Did you read it?"

"Yeh. It was . . . nice."

"Thought you'd like a little external validation." She sits down on an upturned crate. Says this like it's nothing. Maybe it is.

"You know me so well." I pick up a new vessel to work on. Then, "Wait, what does *that* mean?"

She shrugs. "You like the external validation. Have a hard time doing it on your own."

"Loaded but fair. Doesn't everyone?"

"Some more than others."

Now I feel judged. And deflect this by saying (ironically?): "Judgy."

"With love." She gestures like she's bowing to me.

I smooth the vessel's side with a shell. "Ah, judgment tempered by love. My favourite kind."

"Sooo," she starts (uh-oh). "I was thinking of going to visit Shannon."

"Aaaah." (AH!!!!!)

She waits.

"Okay." Because I think I'm supposed to say this. (Not okay!)

She keeps looking. "What do you think of that?"

"I think," I start with a deep sigh, "as long as you're safe, your relationships with others are none of my business." (Not what I think.)

"I don't want to make you mad."

That stops me. I look at her. My beautiful kid. "Mad is not what I am."

"Sad then."

"You don't have to worry about me being sad."

"I do though."

"Well, that makes me sad." I inhale long. Don't want to cry. "I'm your mom. You don't have to worry about me or making me anything."

"Sorry. I love you and don't want you to be sad. It's 'cause I care about you."

I am slow, with my words. With my hands. This vessel. "I don't want you to, you know, have to care too much."

"Pffft. Like you'd let me."

I smirk. "Fair."

"I know it was hard for you when Shannon left and this now, the baby, must be hard too." (Who made this human?)

I meet her honesty with the best I've got: "It is and it isn't. I mean, I know I didn't want another kid . . ."

"When you got it so right the first time." She knows sarcasm soothes me.

"Right!? And I'm happy they're happy type thing."

"You're saying all the right adult things." She fiddles with an old pot. Something I should soak.

I breathe deep, again. "Just hurts is all."

"Yeh." She talks slow. "I think it just wasn't meant to be, you know?"

I nearly guffaw. "That's a nice way to put it."

"How would *you* put it?" She tilts her head like a therapist (lol).

"Oh doesn't matter. I screwed up a lot."

"What a lot? You just weren't right for each other. Relationships don't have to work out. Sometimes they just don't."

So wise and so simple. "You're young."

"Oh, will I understand when I'm older?" (Yay! Sarcasm.)

"Doubt it. I still don't."

A shrug of her baby bony shoulders. "You take breakups hard. Makes sense with all your abandonment trauma." She's not looking at me but at some pots on shelves. Some good ones over there. Her beautiful hair, small hands, the side of her cheek turned to the light.

I smile deep. "Get out of here with your abandonment trauma. Go play outside. Play a video game. Be a kid. Abandonment trauma, pfft." I hope this works. "When are you going?"

"I dunno. Tomorrow, next day? They just said to walk over whenever."

"Walk over?! They're close?"

My kid nods. Has a knowing smile (or is that something else?).

"Hey, my kid," I call as she starts up the stairs. "Did you see baby's name?"

"Oh yeh . . ."

I keep forming vessel 68. Waiting.

"So stupid, hey?" (Sooo my kid.)

June

lyn follows up the sent article with a phone call: "It's good, isn't it? I think it's good."

I stammer back, "Yeh, it's nice. I mean, it's all true and we knew all along and you did something about it so that's good. We look good."

"So?"

"What? You think I should stop worrying?"

"You said it, not me."

"I can't help it. I always worry and think it's all my fault."

"I do that too."

"Oh, I know *you* do." I laugh, maybe a bit too hard.

But she doesn't. "What's *that* mean?"

I laugh again, but more awkwardly. "I'm talking about Shannon."

"Why are you talking about Shannon?!" Pissed. Or just curious. I can't tell.

I think of retracting but naw, she should hear this: "Because you're still blaming yourself up about that."

"I screwed up. I get to process that."

"You're not processing shit. You're feeling bad about yourself. Assholes be assholes, it's not your fault."

"One, you're one to talk, Dr. Anxiety! And two, Shannon wasn't an asshole."

It's on now! "Shannon was *such* a fucking asshole. Shannon was the biggest asshole in a long line of fucking assholes. I'm sorry, lyn, but it's true."

"For wanting a baby?"

"No, not for wanting a baby. For wanting you to make a baby like right away. As soon as they wanted it, you had to step up like, yesterday. They did everything like that, you had to hop to it immediately or they'd threaten to leave. Fuck. Like how many times did they break up with you?!" When it's on, it's on.

"I dunno," she says too quiet. Did I go too far? "They were, they are, a determined kind of person."

"Fuck that." But my voice is more gentle. "They were being childish. Like every time you fought, every single time, they'd break up with you. And you'd call me crying they were going to leave you and you didn't know what to do. You know how hard it was not to say, 'Let them go. Do that, please. Let them the fuck go!'"

"That's not fair. It was their defensive mechanism. They've been traumatized."

"So have I. So have you. You know what my defensive is? I tell Sigh he's being an ass and I go for a walk, or go eat ice cream. I don't threaten to tear down our life every time he pisses me off. Shannon did. And you took all that shit from them and you're still pining and can't let them go."

"I let them go."

"Oh yeh? Really? How many times you creep them and that baby this week?"

"Not one. I've been off everything since all this shit happened."

When I don't say anything:

"No really, I swear." She sounds so broken though.

I sigh. "You're still punishing yourself. You're still beating yourself up for all of it."

"What is this? Why do you always do this picking? Things are good, this article is good, you gotta go look for all the bad." Oh good, she's back.

I take another breath. "I do do that, you're right."

"Yeh, I'm right, trying to fix me. I don't need you to fix me."

Another breath. "I know you're right. You're right. It was a good article."

"It was."

One more and "But fuck Shannon."

"Fuck off."

We're quiet for a long time but neither one of us wants to get off yet. This is a good porch. I have a good porch to sit on and shoot the shit with lyn.

"Ever think this is all Renee's fault?" she says quiet.

"Um duh, yeh," I say to the sky and my treeless view, my sister, the universe. I need a sweater. The sun is leaving. No, we're the ones moving away from the sun.

"No, but like my relationship stuff. With Shannon and well, everyone before them."

"You think everything is Renee's fault. But yeh, in a way, I guess."

"It's like, she was the first. She made us work for love from her. So now we think we have to work for love with everyone."

"I don't think I have to work for love."

"You think you have to work for *everything*."

Contrite: "Nothing comes from nothing."

"See, there you go. We're the saps who think they have to work for everything. Imagine being the kind of person who thinks they just deserve it all."

"Twice as hard for half as much, as Dad would say, right. We have to work hard to get less. That's the Indigenous reality."

"I wonder what other kinds of people are thinking. Like what validates feeling so . . . deserving. So owed?"

"White supremacy," I say quick because it's always the right answer.

"No, I mean emotionally."

She's going an awfully long time without a funny comment. It's unnerving.

"I thought I was the empathetic one. You're the one who says, 'Who cares?! Let's play with clay. La la la!'"

Did she laugh, a little? "You *are* the empathetic one. That's why I asked you. You have to like, humanize the bad guys all the time. Know why they do what you do. It's your thing. I think it might be why you're so anxious. Now. You never used to be like that. You were so tough when you were a kid."

"No, I wasn't. Just hid it better."

"Yeh. I used to hide my crazy better, too."

I laugh good and proper. "Having empathy doesn't mean not having accountability. I do think it's good to consider people's motivations and try and understand. That's how we stop things, fix things, make them better. I think Renee, people who do things like this, are motivated by so many things. Emotionally, I think it's this belief they don't have enough on their own. Like how

Renee's always needed more attention—that's trauma. But polit-ically, it's about power. She didn't just take anything, she took what she thought she could—that's white supremacy, thinking our culture is something she can put on like a costume and no one would know."

"White supremacy and trauma—the answers to everything." My sister is better at concision than I am.

"Yeh, but we all have trauma. Some of us more than others, but not everyone does shit like this."

Calm: "I think we all have different reactions to trauma. Some of us come out thinking everything we do is wrong, and others, like defensively, think everything they do is right. Or has to be, because if they were a little wrong then they're like, all the way wrong. But maybe this thinking is our problem—we're so busy figuring out the *why* and being empathetic and shit, we lose sight of the *what*. We're still just taking care of her. In the end, it doesn't matter why—she did what she did, that's all that matters. She should own it, that's all, just own it. Apologize and move on."

I have got to get the name of her therapist. "Like any of us are any good at owning our shit."

"I'm great at it, I don't know about you." Aaand, she's back.

We're quiet for a bit, again. One cloud floats by. It's long and grey and light.

She sighs. "Can't believe you said that about Shannon."

"What? The truth?"

"Your truth. Doesn't mean it's true."

"It means I love you. I love *you*, lyn, and I really want you to stop beating yourself up and getting hung up on assholes. Just because you're not perfect doesn't mean they are."

"You're one to talk."

"I know, hey?"

lyn

I put all my vessels into two old boxes, get my camera and take my kid to the park by the river. It's wide and grassy with remnants of the old concrete from the docks, wood pillars poking out of the water. A long slope of cleared land.

"What are we doing here?" Willow whines.

"Just help me," and I tell her how to lay them out, make a circle, four spokes. A centre.

It wasn't perfect. This is just a first. The circle's not circular and the spokes aren't straight, or even. Not really. Eight from the centre. Eight around each curve. Sixty-four.

I take shots out toward the water. The clouds rolling the river running. Fort Gibraltar in the blurry background. A large wooden side fencing, a re-creation itself. Magick hour.

The rain is light but still Willow huffs. Runs under the shelter. Scrolls her phone and sighs, loud.

It thunders in the dusk. Rain grows hard, vessels fill 'til water ripples inside. I keep shooting until:

"I'm hungry!"

"Okay okay, I'm coming. Help me pack up." I had promised fast food.

When we get home, I lay them all out to dry. Put them upside down.

I had never even paid attention to their order or grouping. It was so random.

Sounds like me.

We eat the cheap burgers and finish another show. The ending kind of sucks. Feels like a checklist of all the open plot lines but I still get a little weepy. It was good while it lasted.

"Can I have the rest of your fries?"

"Only because you are you, my child."

Willow looks out the window. "Uh, bad white dog people have a new puppy!"

I turn. A middle-aged woman bends over a very young almost shiny dog who chews on its leash. The woman tugs gently. The puppy pays no attention at all.

"Oh no," I say. "You know what that means, right?"

"Circle of life." Matter-of-factly (so cold!) and she turns back to the sub sub secondary plot wrap-up scene.

I think and, "Maybe we should get a dog."

"You'd never survive a dog." Her mouth full.

"I could so survive a dog!"

"Dogs bug you like, all day. They're super needy. You can't even stand Zeke for too long."

"But they're so cute." I look out at the puppy now picked up by the woman who is no longer looking at it belovedly.

"You should get a bunny," Willow says as intelligently as she says everything. "Bunnies are quiet and leave you alone. Take years to warm up to humans, if ever."

"Same."

"True story."

Next time I should take the vessels to my favourite place along the Seine. The place where I harvested the clay they are made of. Earth to earth.

8 is a number that doesn't get as much attention but it's pretty sacred (maybe even the sacredest?). There are 8 doorways in a Midewiwin lodge. 8 is 4 × 2, and 4 is the number of all the things and balance (so 8 is like super balance?). 8 is infinity, the symbol of the Michif people and of course the 8th fire prophecy, which is complicated but one of its meanings is the 8th generation post contact, that generation is the one that heals. Or starts the real healing, depending on who you ask. That's not our generation, we're number 7. 7 is its own special number if you count things like the 7 Grandfather Teachings, but 8 is the OG. Real tradish. We're not the healers, we just, like all generations do, care and prepare for the next one.

Feelings will pass. Are already passing. Like water they change, all the time.

What they make is what lasts, what they leave behind.

8

The People Who
Own Themselves

June

Sigh is hammering away downstairs and I can't think. My sister texts right when I am considering all the places I would put the hammer, if given half the chance.

You want to come over? Get a bottle. Invite Yoyo.

Hell yeh.

"I'm leaving," I call as I walk down the stairs. Zeke follows me but sulks over to his other human when I don't lift the leash.
"Forever?" He doesn't look up at me but does pat the dog.
"Naw, just going to lyn's."
"Thank god."
"You going to be done any time soon?"
"Define done?"
"An actual kitchen?"
"Define soon?"

I close the front door gently, for the sake of the door. There are two new deliveries there. I kick them, a little too hard. More toys. Then stomp across the porch.

We're really gonna have to fight about that soon.

We sit quiet on the deck. lyn sits like someone full of peace and gazes out into the nothing. I scroll my phone. We also both eavesdrop on her neighbours as they splash in their new hot tub and natter at each other like only happily married people can natter at each other.

Finally, Yoyo storms through the house, calling, "My sisters!!" like someone who's arrived at a party and not just to us. She bounds out the back door with a tall bottle of vodka, paper bag full of mix and chips and a long-winded narrative about why and how and all the things she had to do to get here. The couple next door grow quiet. Taking their turn to eavesdrop, maybe.

Our baby sister plops down on the wood beside the small table, talking about traffic, her neighbours, her boyfriend as she piles all her things out and pulls out a pipe.

"You guys saved me from a hell of a lab. Maarsii, mes soeurs." She lights up.
 lyn: "You have to bring dill pickle? No one likes dill pickle."
 "Everyone likes dill pickle, you're just old."
 "What does old have to do with it?"
 "I dunno. Maybe your tastebuds are going or something."

They tease and natter and I try to clear my thoughts. I made the mistake of going online while we waited. Another asshole white supremacist using this as an excuse to talk about race-based bullshit. I check our hashtags again, but no one has flagged us. I want to say something but only the exact right thing.

"Here, June. Drink." lyn hands me a poured glass, mixed exactly how I like it. "Stop thinking." She nudges me, knowing me. "Yoyo, tell her a joke. No, tell her about your dead bodies."

"Oh I have dissected all sorts of dead bodies. This one time . . ."

I try and smile. I smile bigger. I take another long gulp. Yoyo smokes too fast. Even lyn takes a hit.

After a couple passes around the circle, Yoyo really gets into it. She loves some cadavers and hearts but her favourite is blood. "You don't really see the blood like going around in the cadavers, 'cause you know, they're dead, I mean it's there but you're not seeing all it can do. The way it flows, like all over, everywhere. And you know what it looks like? What I always think of? It's like rivers! Blows your mind the way it branches off and does little swirly whirly for seemingly no reason but there is a reason, veins need to be long and flexible to go around and move and, and, give life to everything."

lyn, coughing: "Jesus Christ, Yo, you just blew my mind!"

"I know, I know. It blows my mind too!"

"No, I mean I'm thinking about this project I'm doing, with the vessels and the rivers and water and I think, that's it. It's blood. It's blood and it's Mother Earth and humans!" She shakes Yoyo's side, all excited. "It's us!"

"I know! Yes yes. We are like that, all of us."

"No, it's the land and the body. Together. We are both sovereign."

"We are sovereign sacred beings." Yoyo nods solemnly.

Me: "You are high as fuck!"

And they laugh long.

lyn: "God, I hope I remember that in the morning."

Yo: "You should go write it down. I write down everything on my phone. I always think of great things when I'm not like, working, so I need to."

"That's a good idea, but where's my phone?"

"How do you always lose your phone? I never lose my phone. You always lose your phone. That's definitely an old person thing."

Me: "You're right. You never lose your phone. You're so lucky." But no one picks up my sarcasm.

Yo: "Oh, it's okay, Juney. Are you okay, Juney? Is she okay?"

"She's just mad because Renee is crazy."

"Oh I know, Renee is cuckoo." She whistles the sound, or tries to.

Me: "We should be nicer, you guys. Every being suffers. She's going through a lot, been through a lot."

lyn, nodding too long: "But she's also put us through a lot."

"She was a kid, what did she know?"

Suddenly mad: "I think she knew a bit more than she let on, but whatever. I mean, I managed to raise a kid while being young, traumatized and fucked up and still didn't put my kid in harm's way every chance I got. But whatever."

"I know."

"Don't try and make me feel guilty just 'cause that's all you feel."

Yo: "It's true she's guilty feeling, isn't she? Poor June. Poor widdle Juney."

"Yo, stop!" I can be firm, too.

lyn: "You have nothing to feel guilty for. You think Renee feels guilty? About any of it? Us? You? Me? Impersonating a culture she knows isn't hers? Putting us in constant danger? Stealing Dad's stories? You think she feels guilty about any of it? No, she doesn't. She sleeps like a baby. Telling herself it's all someone else's fault. You're feeling all the guilt for her."

Yo: "Oh man, lynnie, you just blew my mind. She *is* feeling all the guilt for her. That's what, that's what we do sometimes. I think I do that . . ."

I wait for her to finish, but she doesn't. So: "I just think we should, I don't know, forgive her?"

Scary mad: "How can you forgive someone who doesn't think they did anything wrong?"

I have no answer for this.

Yo starts: "You know my friend Aruba?"

"No."

"Like the place . . . ?"

"No wait, waitwaitwait wait, so Aruba? She like *lived* at our house when we were growing up?"

lyn, exasperated: "Neither of us lived there then."

Me, confused: "I was in another country altogether."

"Well anyway, you've both met her dozens of times. Anyways, Aruba and I were to-the-death besties. I loved that chick so bad. Would have given her my arm I loved her so much. I mean, she was messed but I loved her."

"Does this have a point, Yo? You're very high. I—"

"Shhh, listen. So a couple years ago we go to the Dominican. Saved up so long—spring break, awesome, right? And we share a room and we drink for days and I hooked up with a local and it was a really good time. Long before Matt, of course."

lyn: "Of course."

Me: "Of course!"

"But then I get home and unpack and my Kylie palette is like, nowhere."

Me: "What's a—"

lyn: "It's eyeshadow."

"Oh!"

"Man, you guys are old. Anyways, it's nowhere and I text her and she's like I don't know and whatever, I think I left it there. And oh well, too bad but I'll buy a new one, right? I'm fine. Until the next Friday and we go to Cool Bar and I see she has Marigold eyelids and she never had Marigold eyelids before and I'm like, you took my palette! And she's like, I had this palette before you! And I said no you did not! And she's like, you lie! And I'm like, you bitch. So anyways, it got bad, she told everyone I was going crazy and I told everyone she was a liar and a thief and I like never thought I'd talk to her ever again. It went on like that for a couple years. She went total DARVO, classic. And then I got into med school and everyone was like, yay good for you way to go. It was all over my socials so of course she saw and then she even messaged me, all cool and mature and like, I'm so happy for you and whatever like nothing happened, and I could have been a bitch but I decided not to. I mean life's too short, so we started chatting and I, you know, we're cool now. Like we're okay."

"So you're saying forgive and bygones and all that?"

"Well sort of but you know, you gotta let time go for a bit, you know."

I think about this. "Yeh, that's the problem with Renee, there's always another thing to get over, never enough time in between things."

But Yo is on a roll. "Yeh maybe. Like I know Aruba didn't have a lot and did what she did for whatever. I know that but she never like owned up to it. She never will."

"That's what I mean. How do you forgive someone who doesn't think they did anything wrong?"

"You don't forgive people for them, you forgive them for you." She points hard at her own chest. "You do it so you can stop harping on it. Stop letting it all affect you." Her hands wave in the air. Talking like Grandma when she gets going. "That's what I did for Aruba and I feel loads better. I didn't even ever say anything to her, I just did it in here"—she pats her chest—"and it was like a weight was lifted." Air, again.

Me: "You're oddly super wise, wee Yoyo."

She doesn't miss a beat. "This is what I tell people."

I smile at my baby sis. "So we gonna see Aruba again some-day?"

lyn: "Yeh, we all gonna go to Cabo this winter or something?"

"Oh hell no. I am not letting that bitch anywhere near my stuff ever again. I'm not a moron. I can be nice to her but no."

"She's very wise, is our Yoyo," lyn says and pats her on the arm.

Willow pops her head out. "Just letting you know I'm home."

Yo: "Willie girlie!"

"Oh my baby." lyn is too high. "How are you? How did it go?"

"How did what go?"

"She went to see Shannon."

Yo: "No shit!"

lyn whispers for no reason: "And the baby."

"No *shit!*"

My sister reaches for her daughter's hand and takes it lovingly. "How did it go?"

"It's fine, he's fine, he's cute," Willow stammers. So many reasons to be awkward and gently pulls back her hand.

lyn nods, a lot. "I'm glad. Proud of you."

Yo adds with closed eyes: "So proud of you, Willie girl. I love you."

"Love you too, Aunty." Willow backs her way to the door. "I'm going to bed."

"Love you!" her mom calls. "I love her so much."

Yoyo drapes her arms over lyn's legs. "I know you do. We all do." They're both crying. I take the vodka inside, make another drink and then put the bottle out of sight.

By midnight, my sisters dance around the fire, arms up like they're making magick. I finally made it for them after several of their useless attempts. I also filled two buckets of water and put them close by. They're playing that Taylor Swift song for the billionth time and I really need to sleep. It's a good fire. It'll die down in about half an hour. They'll probably still be going though.

I text Sigh to come get me and gaze into the flames while I wait. I love the way fire dances. Draws you in. The sky above and behind it is purple, cloudless. Colder than when we came out.

My husband moseys in with the dog and Yoyo corners him for ten minutes, teasing and laughing. Even lyn gets in on it. I burrow into Zeke's warm fur while they talk about nothing. Eventually, Sigh nudges me. "Let's get you home."

We go slow. My man usually walks in quick stomps and Zeke always wants to run but they both move with me right now.

"You okay?"

"Yeh." And I think, wonder if that's true.

I lean my head on his shoulder and inhale him. His regular day smells. Deodorant, coffee, our house no matter where we are and what state it's in, it always smells like that, like him.

"They're just all here. Like right here."

"Yeh. Weird, hey?

"So weird. I've been away so long. I just, I don't know if I can handle all of them right here all the time."

"But even when you were away, they were still with you. You were never very far. Not really."

"Is that how you feel now? Being away from home again?"

"Oh hell yes. I talk to my mom every day."

"You are a mama's boy."

"You know it."

He looks down at me. I can feel it without looking. "You can do this, June. I promise."

"You can promise that, can you?"

"For sure. I can do anything and I can make all the promises. You don't even know what I can do."

I laugh. Lean in a little more. See our house up ahead.

lyn

I had checked my socials. Finally. After I got off the phone with June and sat there waiting for them to come over. I felt, I don't know, ready? I was feeling cocky, is what it was.

The notifications were bright and red but easy to skip. The DMs a long string of faces as unknown as all those numbers that keep calling.

Mostly reporters, but that gallery owner did message the article ahead of its publication, wanting me to know.

There were seven from Renee,

Mostly very long,

Posted from most recent so it was like last time in reverse.

The last one started you won't be hearing from me again but followed with about three paragraphs about why. I didn't read it.

The next one started by calling me *miserable*. That's all I saw, that word, and stopped reading. It was pretty long but I scrolled and the words blurred.

One of them I saw compared me to ShitFace, Creepy, even CokeHead (yes, the one who tried to kill her), saying she felt abused by me. I had seen their names, all lined up there, a list. A list she put me on. I only read that section.

The first one started with What have I ever done to deserve this? and went on for a long time. That one seemed the most gentle, the rest, the elevated anxiety when I didn't respond, seemed to get more and more angry.

There were so many words and I didn't even read beyond the first lines.

Willow came out to tell me she was going, and I barely responded. But something jarred me as she closed the door. I walked out to the deck and sat in what was left of the warm sun. There were two clouds in the whole sky. So close they were almost one.

I wanted to answer. Felt compelled to just . . . say something, even though I didn't know what.

I thought about Willow's advice to June, of separating the two things—your family relationship with someone and your sense of self, your brand, as she called it. Thought of my sister's anger and guilt. My own anger and how it never went away.

Finally, I went with,

It sounds like you're triggered. That's understandable in all this. I hope you're getting the help and support you need.

(My therapist would have been so proud.)

I held my breath as the blue dots rose and fell then rose again.

Fell again.

Didn't come back up.

Funny, all this time I thought it was me not talking to her.

There was another person's message way down the list when it all first came out.

Hey. I am so sorry all this is happening, lyn. If you need anything at all, just let me know. I hope you're taking care. [winky face, blushing face, red heart]

It was posted late at night. At the end of our long relationship thread. They would have seen it all too, when they put it up there, out there. Harmless to the untrained eye, but more, maybe. Sometimes. I used to call it checking their traps. Notes sent out like sticky tape for flies, metal teeth for wolves, trying to catch.

I scrolled through the missed calls but didn't see their number. The one I deleted but thought I still knew. It's not there. Could be the same. Could try it.

No, it was better this way. The message there. Nothing more. I don't even have to respond. I don't have to do anything.

I sat out on the deck in the slow gathering of night. Nothing but the birdsong and slow wait for my sisters to come over. The neighbours turned their hot tub on. A drone sound that quieted everything else.

I read their message one more time. (Three more times.) Then deleted it all. The whole thread gone away made invisible like it didn't even happen at all. I felt it go. Felt the space it used to hold, made empty.

Deleted all Renee's too. Then all the reporters and gawkers asking nosy questions.

The only ones left were the friends, the real ones asking for nothing at all only wondering how I was. I will answer them tomorrow.

I sat there for a long time (my sisters are always late), I felt a million feelings. Didn't beat myself up at all.

June

One morning I go for a run, take Zeke. We go up Garbage Hill and barely feel the incline. I run around the top awhile and make my dog happy. I do hate running though.

I sit at a shaded park bench and give Zeke some water. He sits under me, leaning his whole weight on the backs of my calves.

I find her name in my contact list. It rings three times.

"Well! To what do I owe this honour?"

"Hi, Renee."

"Hi, yourself. I thought"—her anger cracks a little—"thought you were done with me."

"No, Renee, I'm not done with you. I was upset though. Still am, if I'm honest."

"I get that you have to, you know, save face and all that. The mob is going real crazy with all this. But to act like you had no idea. The words you said. Hurt me so much, Juniper. So much."

I sigh. Swallow my usual I know I know. My usual acknowledgement. And choose: "All of this hurt me too, Renee. It hurt so many people. What you did, saying what you've said. All of it. It's stealing, Renee. It's pure theft. It's, you took Dad's stories.

You took his life, the things that happened in his life, in my life, lyn's life, and pretended they were yours. You pretended and you stole. With no understanding of how unjust, how just plain not right it is." I sigh a huff. I really huff.

"Well, sounds like you had that ready for a while. Feel better now?"

"No, Renee, I don't feel better. Nothing about this is ever going to feel better. I hate, I hate all of this. I hate that I didn't do anything. I hate that you did this. I hate that you do this. I hate it all."

She takes a deep breath. I can feel her trying to decide on what tactic to try. She ends up with, "This isn't about you, Juney girl. This is my life. My whole life that just got an atomic bomb thrown at it. I have lost everything." Indignant with a side of victim.

"You were living a lie."

"No, I wasn't. You don't understand. This is me. My truth!" Loud indignant.

"Then why did you steal Dad's stories? If it's so true, why did you have to lie?"

"You always believe your dad over me. One day you will grow up and realize he's not perfect." Deflecting.

"Dad is not perfect, I know that. But he is Indigenous. I know that too."

"You've always been such a spiteful girl. You're not the only one who gets to be all special, you know." Cutting. Biting. Aiming to hurt.

I try and keep my voice as level as possible. "You don't get to be Indigenous just because you want to. You do realize that, don't you?"

She lets out another loud sigh. This is her most used tactic, to treat us like her clueless children and her the ever-patient mother. "June. I love you. But you don't understand."

"But I do, Renee. I teach this stuff. I have degrees in this stuff. I write about it all the time. I know our people, our history, the actual truth, not just what I want to be true. We come from here, and we are a culture born out of generations of people working together, making things together, doing things together. We're not upstarts who discovered some distant Indigenous ancestor from years ago and think that makes us Indigenous too. We're not people who have grown and lived with immense white privilege, because they are in fact white, who think they are entitled to something, to feel special, as you say. I am not who I am because I feel it, I am who I am because I know it, and I know my father and his father and his father before him. I am Michif because I am. You are not Michif or Métis, you just wish you were."

When she says nothing: "You don't get all the good and none of the bad. It doesn't work that way."

"You don't know how good you've had it. I didn't have half the so-called privilege you had."

"That still doesn't make you Indigenous."

"And your dad's family, well, they had a lot too. My family was so much poorer." Cornered and lashing.

"And that still doesn't make you Indigenous."

"I got where I am with my talents, my skills."

"Appropriating art that didn't belong to you. Wearing my culture as a costume because you thought it would get you something."

"I have worked hard. You don't know how hard I have worked." Her voice slows and breaks.

"That still doesn't make you Indigenous."

She's quiet. Thinking loudly. "You said here. Are you home?"

"Yeh. We're here now."

"And you weren't even going to tell me . . ." Breaking. Saddened.

"I'm telling you now."

"What did I ever do to make you hate me so much?"

"I don't hate you, Renee."

"Well, you sure act like it."

"I am only saying what I've been avoiding saying. What I haven't had the courage to say. To you."

She sniffles. "Courage, hey? That's what you call it. You do have guts, I'll give you that. You get that from me." Almost a chuckle. A softening. Cloying.

"Yeh, I probably do."

"Anyways, I don't care a bit. I'm over this, pardon my French, shit and this city. All of it. The art world can go fuck itself. I'm moving to the West Coast. I'm going to be a yoga teacher."

I laugh. Like really laugh. From my gut.

lyn

I take June out to the river on a Saturday afternoon. My vessels carefully wrapped in sturdy boxes, placed with care in the back of my car. I drive to a brief clearing. Barely a clearing, mostly bush. The creek of a river shines brown in the grey light of the fall day.

I walk gently and place each pot in the tall grass. It feels like it's going to rain. It's so cold that would feel like ice. Could turn to snow at this rate. I am not ready for winter.

I make eight spokes out, all random, all a different number of vessels long. Some have as few as four pots, one peters off toward the river, sixteen on that one.

When they feel right, I crouch down to shoot. Lie in the grass even, to get the shots. The leaves sulk on thin trees. The creek rumbles as the rain starts to fall. I was right, it does feel like ice.

June shivers so I throw her the car keys. By the time I follow, the heat is blasting.

"We gotta wait for it to rain awhile," I say.

"I am freezing."

I only side-eye her.

"Wanna get some food?"

"I made a couple sandwiches, if you want." I motion to the bag on the back seat.

She begrudgingly unwraps a peanut butter one. Out of nowhere: "So you seeing anyone these days?"

I laugh. "God no! Why?"

"Because love is love and it's what people do. It's going to be a cold fucking winter."

"Meh."

"You gotta stop being hung up on that asshole."

She stings me. "We all can't have your perfect marriage, you know."

"It's not perfect!" she answers too quick.

"Sure looks like it."

"It's been, it's not always been easy."

I scoff. "What, that colleague? Sigh's annoying toys? That's really all the problems you got, isn't it?"

"No, not just that." Both of us feeling sensitive today, I guess. She inhales. "Sigh spends money like a motherfucker and I'm pretty sure he's going to spend all we've got because he thinks credit is like, free money, and then I will really have nothing."

"Yeh, right."

"It fucks with my sense of security."

"You don't feel secure because you don't have access to thousands of dollars? You know how privileged that sounds. I'm lucky if I have hundreds in the bank. Tens even. Plus, you have a big fancy job."

"Now. Finally. And I hate it. And it hasn't even started yet. It means I'm stuck here and I can't screw up because no one would hire me again, so I have to work in an institution that literally made up the term settler colonialism."

"So I'm supposed to feel sorry for you because you have a good job?"

"I'm not asking you to feel sorry for me. I'm just telling you I'm not perfect."

"I know *you're* not perfect, but your life looks pretty perfect."

"What about *your* life? You're free. You could absolutely go anywhere, do anything, take your kid and have an adventure. You're so fucking full of freedom and you stay here."

"I like it here."

"Bullshit."

"I am doing work here." My hands wave out over my project.

"You could work anywhere."

"Why you turning this on me?"

"Same reason you're picking on me."

"Fine."

"Fine!"

I go out again when the rain starts to sleet and the grey clouds roll over, reflect in the water. I shoot from the ground out, so the river blurs in the distance. I go show them to my sister when she won't come out of the car.

"Have you talked to her since then?" I say when we grow quiet.

She huddles in her jacket despite burning all my gas over-heating the car. "Naw. I doubt I will."

"Pretty ballsy talking to her like that. You must feel guilty."

"Naw. I mean naw. I do but I also don't, you know."

"Yeh? Wow. Good for you."

"Yeh, I'm trying to . . . let it go. Let it be."

"Good plan. Either way."

We don't say anything for a long time. It gets dark and I think I should go. Pack up and take my sister home. She looks fried.

"You know"—her chin in her sweater—"I think I was so tough as a kid because I was protecting you."

"Me? Aw, that was nice of you."

"I'm a nice person."

I grin, literally grin. "I have always said that about you. So so nice."

She sighs. "I am doing what you always say, trying to let myself feel sad about it. Feel sad and do nothing. Just, you know, grieve."

"Good for you."

"It fucking sucks."

"Does."

"I drink a lot of wine."

"Gotta support wineries. Local businesses and all that."

"And I've been running."

"Whatever gets you through the night."

"It sucks."

"Yeh, I do miss the comforting numbness of disassociating all the time, but they say this is better." At least I still have the joy of sarcasm.

"I call bullshit."

"I hear you."

"I just really want her to find peace, you know. I really want that for her." My sister's voice low. Darker now. I can't see her face anymore.

"Yeh," I say to the night.

"I want that for us, too."

"I think I'm going to make more for next time." I point my chin to my vessels the land the water. "Maybe a winter one. I want to align them with the stars. Maybe at Oodena Circle at Nestawaya. That's a summer solstice alignment, hey?"

Out of nowhere: "We should write a book together!"

"What? No."

"Why not? We have all this knowledge, we can put it all together."

"Who says it goes together?"

"Sure it does. It can be about Michif-ness and history, and ancient history and vessels and things relearned. Something about trauma obviously because there's always trauma, unfortunately, but mostly about post-trauma, the getting over of things, the healing part. The ongoing nature of the story, how we're only now in the middle of things. It could be about pretendians and identity, too. And art! We could totally break it all open, defy convention, say it all how we want to—belonging, family, being true to ourselves, our people, as best we can."

"Sounds like a mess."

"Well, we're messy. But we're also real!"

"We are that." I think on this a beat or two. All the things we could do. "Hey, we should do a road trip, all the Circles near here. I could take pictures and you could, I don't know, do what you do."

"That would be beautiful. I've been to the one in Alberta but yeh, I'd love to see the rest. We could go in spring."

"No, summer, best road trips are in summer. We could see the Wild West stuff too. Ironically, of course."

My sister laughs. "Of course. I could write a grant application, get that all covered."

I lean over: "Guuurl, now you are speaking my language."

"It'll be great." She smiles. "We'll make millions."

"June, this is Canada. We'll be lucky if we make hundreds."

"Hundreds, then. Good thing I have that fancy job."

"You're still going to write the grant though, right?"

"Sure, as long as you buy me a tea. I am freezing my balls off."

"Amateur."

She gets out with me to pack up. The cold rain lets up as we work but the sky doesn't clear. The car lights show us where to go.

I put down the boxes and show my sister how to stack them carefully. Everything in reverse and so mindful. She handles them delicately, like they're rare precious artefacts already.

Maybe they are.

Acknowledgments

A book always needs a village, but this one in particular felt like it needed an army.

In no particular order:

Marilyn Biderman and Nicole Winstanley. Meredith Pal, Dan French and everyone at Penguin.

Julie Flett and Jennifer Griffiths, for creating the most amazing cover.

KC Adams, whose practice inspired lyn's and who just happens to inspire me all the time.

Laura Forsythe, for reviewing early excerpts, Chantal Fiola and Brenda Macdougall, whose work in particular inspired June's and whose Michif power is changing the world for the better.

Michelle Porter, for a conversation that healed something in me and fixed something in this book.

Michelle Good, who knows more about pretendians than they know about themselves and who said the epigraph—"truth is like water . . ."—during one of our long-winded phone conversations early on in my writing of this. Those words have stayed and shaped things in so many ways.

Michelle Cyca, for reviewing this manuscript and offering thoughts, and for all her warrior work.

Chrysta Swain, Anna Lundberg, Vanda Fleury, and all my bitches, my makeshift coven. I love you.

Alo Mide'Kiwenzie, Peter White, and to Carla, too. You honour me.

My kids, my nieces, my brother, father, and mother. My imperfect perfect family.

My therapists, current and former, who I will not name because they know too much.

All the many books, articles, podcasts that have taught me, filled the gaps and kept me going. I make a (completely incomplete) bibliography for every book but this one had four: therapy, ancient history, Michif history, and pretendians. (Shortest answer: I highly recommend reading the work of Steven C. Hayes, Paulette Steeves, Jean Teillet and Kim TallBear—respective to those four reading lists, but there are so many others.) Maarsii, good people, for all you've done to make this human experience all the more mind-blowing.

My rivers for keeping me, my city for holding me close, my dogs for making sure I walk, my cats for making sure I nap.

I am sure I have forgotten many, many others. Forgive me, this is a daunting process that takes years.

Finally, and especially, Chi Miigwetch to our ancestors for dreaming us and making sure we came true.